37 PEASES POINT WAY

SISTERS OF EDGARTOWN SERIES

KATIE WINTERS

37 Peases Point Way
Sisters of Edgartown Series
By
Katie Winters

CHAPTER ONE

————————

AMELIA TAYLOR'S schedule was always jam-packed, with her mind racing at its standard setting of a million thoughts a minute. It was yet another Monday morning in early March, and her beige trench coat swirled out behind her as she rushed to her car. There was nothing Amelia Taylor couldn't do, nothing she couldn't conquer.. She had enough time for everyone and everything.

As she stepped on the gas, she pondered her schedule. A meeting regarding the repairs for the Edgartown swimming pool in just twenty minutes; then, a road-worker meeting regarding the approval of a bill to fix up the many potholes prior to tourist season; after that, her day planner screamed out a number of other meetings, a lunch with an important Edgartown figure, all before evening, when she'd collapse on the bleachers of the high school for her niece's cheerleading competition. She'd be the loudest clapper in the audience. After all, Mandy's father couldn't make it and

Amelia was something of a stand-in mom. Mandy had to know she cared.

Five minutes later, Amelia parked in the lot at the Frosted Delights Bakery. She hurried inside, grateful to find Jennifer Conrad at the register.

"You're here! I was worried you would be at the office this morning," Amelia said.

"I thought I would be, too, but Connie called in sick again," Jennifer said. She rushed around to the front to swallow Amelia in a hug. Jen's red tresses stirred alongside Amelia's dark ones. Amelia had always been secretly jealous of Jennifer's red hair — although being the tiniest bit jealous of Jennifer Conrad's looks was something of a Martha's Vineyard obsession. The fact that Jennifer's husband, Joel, had wanted a divorce had totally thrown Amelia off. Of course, Jennifer had met an incredibly hot and rich guy from New York just last December and he'd fallen head-over-heels for her.

How did people do it, Amelia often wondered. How did they hop from love to love, as though they just trusted their own emotions? And it wasn't as though Jennifer was altogether less busy than Amelia, although Amelia liked to use her job as her excuse for the lack of love in her life.

"You're probably in a rush, aren't you?" Jennifer asked. "Can I grab you a coffee? A donut?"

"I don't know about the donut," Amelia said doubtfully.

"Come on, Amelia. I know for a fact you won't have time to eat breakfast. And what will you have for lunch? A side salad with a main course of yet another business meeting?" Jennifer slipped a maple-glazed donut into a little brown baggie and passed it over the top of the counter. She then dotted a to-go cup of coffee next to it.

"You're too good to me," Amelia said.

"You're just not good enough to yourself," Jennifer replied as she furrowed her brow.

"I don't have time for a sermon," Amelia said, grabbing the bag and coffee. "I gotta run. I love you!"

"And I love you, Amelia Taylor!" Jennifer called as Amelia rushed out into the early morning chill. "Take care of yourself!"

Once in the car, Amelia's phone began to blare. She carefully placed the coffee cup in the cup-holder, then answered her phone so that it rang through the speaker system of her car.

"Good morning!" she said as she eased out of the parking lot.

"Amelia, so glad I caught you before the swimming pool meeting." This was her boss, Zane, whom Amelia had never really respected or liked. It was difficult for her to understand why he was her boss, as it seemed he spent most of his working life locked in his office, avoiding the many people of Edgartown who needed him.

"Morning, Zane," Amelia said. Her voice was somber and sterile.

"So the swimming pool people are going to push for a pretty hefty budget. They want to add several more slides and a whole new play-place for kids," Zane said. "I wanted to warn you beforehand."

"Warn me?" Amelia thought back to the swimming pool, which had needed an update for at least ten years. "I think that all sounds good. God knows it gets enough foot traffic during the summertime."

"We haven't budgeted for something like that this year," Zane countered.

Amelia rolled her eyes slightly and adjusted her hands on the steering wheel. She didn't want to get into this argument again; Zane and Amelia had very different ideas of how to budget for the city. He edged more toward the projects that would bring in ritzier clientele, tourists with a lot of cash to throw around. It was true that those weren't the types of people who frequented the Edgartown swimming pool. But the people who did? Islanders. Edgartown kids with nothing to do. That's who Amelia cared about the most.

"I'll just hear them out," Amelia replied. "Maybe it isn't as bad as you think."

"I think you should tell them to reassess," Zane said. "Be strict with them."

"Why don't you come to the meeting yourself? Tell them in person?" Amelia tapped the steering wheel as her nostrils flared.

There was a pregnant pause. If Amelia had to guess, Zane probably wasn't even showered and dressed yet. He kind of eased in and out of the office when he pleased.

"I can't make it this morning."

Of course, he can't.

Amelia was very close to city hall. She paused at the stop sign for a moment and then stepped on the gas. Her eyes were bleary with chill and annoyance. In just two seconds, she would turn left into the parking lot, where her parking spot was located near to the side door, where she could slip in and out easily. When she'd been given the parking spot, she'd thought, wow, I've finally made it. And then, she'd burst into tears because a parking spot was literally an empty plot of land, and that was her reward for working just so dang hard.

"Okay then," Amelia said to Zane. "I'll let you go, then."

But the moment she placed her finger over the button to end the call, it all happened. There was the crunch, then the tip of her car toward the left. She gripped the steering wheel with white fingers and stabbed her foot on the break as she hollered out. She yanked her head to the right to see the car — a Mercedes Benz, which had just struck her corner. It had attempted to come out of a small alleyway and hadn't seen her. To be fair to the driver, there was a massive brick wall between the alley and her direction of the road, which had blocked his field of vision.

Even still, a minor car accident hadn't been on Amelia's schedule.

Amelia grumbled as she made eye-contact with the driver. She pointed toward the parking lot, and he nodded and followed her in so they could assess the damage. The Benz pulled up alongside her, parking in Zane's spot.

Amelia jumped out of the car and stepped around to the right-hand corner of her vehicle to inspect. There the slightest crunch, and the glass of the light had been busted through. She scrunched her nose as the driver who had struck her stepped from his Benz. When her eyes turned up toward his face, her heart thudded in her throat.

He was maybe forty, forty-five, with broad shoulders, dark, salt-and-pepper hair, and piercing, cerulean eyes. He wore an expensive suit beneath a long black trench coat, assuredly also expensive.

"I am so sorry," were the first words that came out of his mouth. His voice was a deep baritone. It sent a shiver down Amelia's spine.

"That brick wall back there — I should have just turned around rather than take a risk."

"I understand," Amelia said. "I've gone out that way before. It's scary."

"I guess you've never wrecked your car doing it, though," the guy said.

"No. True," Amelia said. Her heart slowed as she gazed into his eyes. "But it's not so bad. I have a busted light. And yours?"

They analyzed where his car had struck hers, on the left-hand side, again near the light.

"It's like looking at two puzzle pieces," Amelia said with a laugh.

The guy laughed along with her. "I'm so relieved you're okay. I can't remember the last time I was in an accident. Ten years, maybe? I was driving a clunker back then, so it didn't really matter."

"I think it's been longer for me," Amelia replied, surprised that she and this guy had fallen into such sudden and easy banter.

"You seem way too intelligent and responsible to ever cause an accident yourself," the guy said.

Amelia felt her cheeks warm and prayed that they hadn't actually turned red. *Blushing at forty? Was there anything more embarrassing?*

They exchanged information as Amelia exhaled deeply. There was something so bizarre about any car accident, no matter how serious. It reminded you that at any point, your entire day could be yanked off the rails. It wasn't up to you. It was up to fate.

"Amelia Taylor," the man, whose name was Nathan Gregory, said. He said her name as though it was a beautiful song.

It had been a long time since someone had said her name like that.

"Nathan Gregory," Amelia recited.

"It was a pleasure to bump into you today," Nathan said. His smile was crooked and charming.

In spite of everything, Amelia laughed aloud. "Be careful out there."

"You too. You never know what kind of idiots are ready to jump around corners," Nathan quipped.

Amelia eased a dark curl around her ear. She wondered what she looked like to this man, who'd already told her he was on the island only briefly for a few meetings. He was from Boston. When his eyes connected with hers, her stomach dropped. It had been a long time since she had thought of herself through a man's eyes.

Amelia stepped back toward the door of city hall and watched as Nathan dropped into his Mercedes Benz. There was so much more she was curious about, so much she wanted to ask him about his time on the island and his career, all while gazing into those bright eyes.

But that moment, her secretary hustled out of the side of the building and called her name. "Amelia! Your eight o'clock is all set up and ready in your office. We're all waiting on you."

Nathan nodded, his eyes still latched to hers through the glass of his windshield. Reluctantly, Amelia turned and followed her secretary back through the door. It was time to set herself up for the rest of her day.

But it had certainly been a rather interesting start.

CHAPTER TWO

A FEW MINUTES after Amelia's lunch meeting, her stomach gurgled. She'd hardly had time to pierce through her salad as she'd discussed plans for a new line of docks with more stability, to be purchased and set up prior to summertime's sailing season. She'd watched her salad return to the kitchen, where it had been tossed out into the trash. There had been too much to discuss, too many questions to ask and her hunger had abandoned her, only to return in full-force.

The donut! Amelia reached for the little brown baggie, still in her purse, and removed the maple-glazed wonder. She closed her eyes and took a small bite. The flavors engulfed her tongue as she moaned. At that moment, her phone blared yet again with perhaps the fortieth call of the day. When she glanced at it, however, a very welcome name appeared.

"Camilla!" Amelia said, with bits of donut in her mouth. "You caught me with my mouth kind of full. I'm having an emotional moment with a donut."

Camilla's laughter rang out through her speakerphone. "You mean I actually caught the famously-busy Amelia Taylor outside of a meeting?"

"It's your lucky day," Amelia quipped, leaning back in her chair. "How are you doing?"

"Oh, fine. Just got out of a shift," Camilla returned. There was sadness to her voice, which had lingered there since her husband had left her around Christmas. "Not sure quite what to do with myself the rest of the day. Andrea and I have been busy with wedding planning all week, but she headed back to New York just now. Guess it's another night of microwave burritos and old reruns."

Amelia hated this self-defeated talk from Camilla. Camilla had always been a wonderfully strong, passionate, and intelligent person, even since childhood and into high school, when she had spent a lot of her free time volunteering at the hospital. But a broken heart did horrible things to a person's soul. At least, this is what Amelia had sensed in others; she'd never been in love and, therefore, had never fallen victim to a broken heart.

"I wish I could take you out for a night on the town," Amelia told her. "But Mandy has another cheerleading competition tonight."

"You're always at those cheer competitions. And Jake's ball games."

It was true that Amelia had missed the last few dinners with her best friends, as she'd had family priorities. Camilla, Jennifer, Olivia, and Mila all were, technically, family — but at seventeen and eighteen, respectively, Jake and Mandy just needed her in a different, bigger way. Their mother had been gone a long, long time.

"Don't suppose I can convince you to join me?" Amelia asked. "The concession stand doesn't have any microwave burritos, but they do have killer hot dogs."

"If I remember correctly, their bags of popcorn are more like butter soup," Camilla said with a laugh.

"Yes. You basically have to eat the popcorn with a spoon," Amelia stated. "You should come. There's literally nothing like watching a ton of beautiful and powerful athletes while eating junk food on the sidelines."

"I think you might be right about that," Camilla agreed.

Amelia arrived at the high school gymnasium a bit before the competition was set to begin. She perched on the highest level of the stands and watched as Mandy spoke to several of the other senior cheerleaders, who looked at her earnestly. Mandy was a force of nature: cheerleading captain, A-student, incredibly beautiful, with dark hair that swirled down her back and big, doe-like eyes. She'd made the varsity cheer squad during her freshman year and had elevated her team to an incredible level, allowing them to compete at state the previous two years. Naturally, Amelia had been along for the ride and a proud aunt.

As Mandy wrapped up her pep-talk, her eyes turned toward Amelia. She gave a slight wave, then bounded toward the bleachers to say hello. Amelia was reminded of a much younger Mandy, who'd always seemed wild with energy. As a kid, especially when Amelia had had to watch her and her brother, Jake, after their mother's abandonment, Mandy had wanted to run everywhere she went. Amelia had always called after her to slow down. She'd never really listened.

Amelia met Mandy at the bottom of the stands. When they hugged, sharp, overly flowery perfume assaulted Amelia's nose. When Mandy leaned back, she exhaled and whispered, "I'm so nervous for some reason. Oak Bluffs isn't that bad this year and the team coming down from Falmouth? They have this insanely talented freshman, and their pyramids are just so solid. Ours is still a bit shaky, to be honest." She then leaned forward conspiratorially and said, "We have a sophomore who keeps messing up. I told coach I don't know if she can hack varsity, but now that it's March, it's a little late for that kind of talk, you know?"

Amelia chuckled. She had never been particularly into sports, especially not back in high school, but she had gone to see Jennifer, Michelle, and Mila cheer several times and knew the lingo pretty well. Cheerleaders were some of the toughest athletes around.

"I know you'll do great. You always do," Amelia beamed at her niece.

Mandy shrugged. "You never know."

"True. Oh, I wanted to ask. How did that paper turn out?" About a week before, Amelia had helped Mandy with a school paper for her economics class. They'd stayed up till around two the night before checking all relevant facts. Amelia had been a zombie the next day.

Mandy beamed. "I got an A-minus, actually."

"Yes! That's fantastic!" Amelia lifted a hand for a high-five, which Mandy just shook her head at. Slowly, Amelia returned her hand to her hip. She should have known better than to try that, especially around Mandy's cheerleading squad.

"Yeah. Thank you for your help," Mandy flashed a warm smile. "I better get back to the girls. There's no end to the pep-talks when you're the captain."

Amelia returned to her position on the top of the bleachers as other parents and students arrived. In front of the bleachers, a table was set up, where the judges would sit and rate the three teams. Toward the far end of the gym, a man sat with a microphone in preparation for acting as the announcer for the night. He also worked as one of the radio announcers for the morning radio station based in Edgartown.

"Good evening, ladies and gentleman, and welcome to the twenty-first annual cheerleading competition between Oak Bluffs, Edgartown, and Falmouth High Schools!" he blared a few minutes later.

Just then, Camilla appeared at the base of the bleachers. With one hand, she carried a massive hot dog, covered in bright green relish; with her other, she carried a big tub of buttery popcorn. Her grin was mischievous and Amelia was grateful for it. When was the last time she'd seen Camilla so carefree?

"There you are," Amelia greeted with a smile. "I thought you were bailing on me."

"No way." Camilla sat down next to Amelia and passed over the bag of popcorn. "The line at the concessions stand was insane."

"You can't get between Edgartown's finest and their snacks," Amelia agreed.

"Have a bite of this hot dog," Camilla ordered. "It's seriously sinful."

They settled back together and waited for the main contest to begin. The stands filled up in a matter of minutes, and the air simmered with smells of pizza, hot dogs, buttered popcorn, and soda. Amelia watched as Mandy gave her team yet another pep talk; she bounced on her bright white tennis shoes and beamed at them. This was her very last competition, and she wouldn't accept anything but their best.

"Mandy really grew up, didn't she?" Camilla said with a sigh. "I remember when she was ten and spending all those nights with you. You were so confused. Calling me all the time to ask what girls aged ten liked to eat for dinner."

"I think I went with pizza most nights," Amelia said. "Seemed to do the trick."

"Has Daniel heard anything from their mom lately?" Camilla asked.

"Nope. To be honest, I stalked her social media recently," Amelia said. "I was curious if she was still with that guy. She is. And they live in some high-rise in Manhattan with two dogs. Last year, they went on a cruise through the Mediterranean Sea. It looks like they're doing okay."

"Jeez. You have to wonder what kind of monster would just up and leave her kids without a second thought," Camilla shook her head in disgust. "I can't imagine it. I won't see Andrea for a few weeks this month, and it feels awful."

Amelia didn't have many words for this; after all, she wasn't a mother. She'd never know the bond between a child and their mother. Still, Mandy and Jake were her world and she tried to be there for them as much as she could. Their mother just chose not to and it was really hard to understand that.

Oak Bluffs performed, then Falmouth. Camilla whispered several times that she'd never seen such amazing performances.

Girls flipped wildly, tossed their feet behind their heads, and piled on top of one another for pyramids. Each performance was only between three to five minutes, but it was such intense cardio, it nearly gave Amelia a heart attack.

"I have no idea if that was good or not, but I'm impressed. And exhausted," Camilla said, as Falmouth rushed off the center floor to leave it empty for Edgartown High.

Amelia had seen this senior-year performance several times. It started with a flurry of leaps and backflips and then culminated with a pyramid, which placed Mandy on the second tier, off to the right. Throughout the first few minutes of the performance, Amelia hardly breathed at all. She watched Mandy's precise movements, the way she stuck her arms in the air, then whipped them back for a perfect flip, totally mesmerized.

Then, Mandy placed her foot upon the hands of two of her teammates, who then flipped her through the air. She was meant to whip around and then curve her legs out behind her so that she eventually landed toward the back-end of the gym.

But there was something off about her flip. As she flew, Amelia stood, recognizing that she hadn't gotten herself around in the right way. Suddenly, Mandy landed on her shoulder on the mat, and her legs whacked out beyond her. Immediately, the crowd gasped. The two girls who'd thrust her in the air looked at each other in shock, then guilt. *Had they not sent her out correctly? Whose fault was this?*

Amelia rushed down from the bleachers in a panic. Someone cut the music. She whipped through the other cheerleaders, through a sea of their horrible perfume, and landed alongside Mandy, who held her shoulder and groaned. Her face was horribly pale.

"Mandy! Hey! You're okay. You're okay." Amelia's voice broke as she helped Mandy lay back.

Mandy's eyes found Amelia's. Amelia steadied her expression so that Mandy knew she was safe. The school's sport's doctor arrived beside them to inspect Mandy.

"They pushed me off wrong," Mandy breathed. "I didn't have enough time to get myself back around."

"I know," Amelia said, although, of course, she'd had no idea. "Everyone could see that."

"I'm so embarrassed," Mandy whispered as her lower lip quivered. "This was our last shot."

"We just have to make sure you're okay," Amelia said. Her eyes turned toward the sports doctor. He gave her a nod and then began asking Mandy about her pain levels and about whether or not she could move her arm.

Amelia stood back for a second. Toward the bleachers, Camilla gave her a worried look. Amelia realized she hadn't breathed properly since Mandy had crashed down. She forced herself to inhale, exhale. She then grabbed her phone and made the call no parent ever wanted to receive.

"Hey, sis!" Her brother, Daniel replied, who worked at the Vincent House Museum and had put on a fancy, black-tie event that night for a number of investors. "What's up? I can't talk long."

"Hey Dan," Amelia said. "Um. I just wanted you to know. Mandy had a little bit of an accident."

Daniel's voice changed immediately. "What happened?" he asked, his tone laced with worry. "Where is she?"

"We're still at the gym. I'm trying to get a feel for how bad it is. If she's cleared to go home, I'll bring her right back to yours."

"Okay. I can get out of here in the next half-hour or so," Daniel replied.

"Good."

"And Amelia?"

"Yeah?"

"Thank you so much for being there. I mean that. I have no idea what me and the kids would do without you."

"Of course. I don't know what I would do without you three, either." Amelia's voice broke the slightest bit. Her brother did go out of his way to show his gratefulness, and each time, Amelia made sure to translate just how much they meant to her, too.

She'd never fallen in love. She'd never had children. It had never been her time. And frequently, she had told herself that maybe, this was God's plan for her. Mandy, Jake and Daniel needed her. That had to be enough.

CHAPTER THREE

THANKFULLY, Mandy was cleared to return home with Amelia. Somberly, pouting, Mandy led Amelia back into the locker room, where Amelia collected Mandy's school supplies. She carried them out to the car so that Mandy could continue to press an ice pack against her shoulder. When they reached the parking lot, Camilla eased by in her car and waved to them both. Amelia was grateful Camilla hadn't stuck around. There just wasn't anything to say to Mandy, who was borderline heartbroken over tonight's incident.

When they reached Amelia's vehicle, she opened the car door as Mandy assessed the damaged light. Amelia had all-but-forgotten about the morning incident.

"What happened?" Mandy asked as she slid into the front seat carefully.

"Some guy hit me," Amelia said. "This morning. He couldn't see me and he just ran out in front of me. It happened in a flash."

Mandy made a weird sound in her throat. "Maybe today is cursed or something."

"Maybe," Amelia agreed.

Daniel had moved his children and wife into this house back when their lives had been cookie-cutter perfect — beautiful wife, gorgeous and happy children, all the love in the world. When Amelia pulled up in front of the familiar sight, she again marveled at Suzy's ability to take off one day and never look back.

"Here we are. Home sweet home," Amelia turned, smiling at her niece.

"Great," Mandy grumbled.

At the door, Amelia slid her spare key into the lock and opened it. Jake burst out from the kitchen; his eyes were large. He was seventeen, athletic, and his hair was all tousled and wild. He wore only a pair of sweatpants and a stained t-shirt. His lips were speckled with red sauce.

"What happened to you?" he asked.

"Shut up, Jake," Mandy returned.

"Just a little accident," Amelia said. "What are you eating?"

"Frozen pizza," Jake said, turning from the doorway. "There's more."

"I think we should order better pizza," Amelia said. "Mandy, why don't you go change? Your dad should be home soon."

Mandy grumbled as she retreated down the shadowy hallway toward her bedroom. After she kicked the door closed, loud music swarmed out from under it. Amelia adored these kids — of course, she did. But they hadn't avoided teenage moodiness.

"What happened," Jake asked under his breath as Amelia

looked up the number of their favorite pizza place, Edgartown Pizza.

"They threw her wrong," Amelia whispered. "She's pretty mad, to say the least."

"Damn. And that was her last contest as a senior...." Jake breathed.

"Language, Jacob," Amelia hissed, just as Edgartown Pizza answered the phone. "Hello! Yes. I'd like to make an order for delivery?"

———

IT WAS a lot like any other night at the Taylor household. In time, Mandy limped out from her room and admitted her shoulder felt a whole lot better; Daniel returned from the museum to listen to the war stories from the competition; Jake ate more than his fair share of the pizza, and Mandy picked a fake fight about it. Amelia fell into the fun banter; she teased Jake about his hair and her brother for his funny, Italian suit, which he always wore for these fancy evenings at the museum.

As Jake recounted something that had happened at his basketball practice earlier that day, Amelia's phone buzzed. She didn't recognize the number but had been expecting a call from one of the contractors she'd spoken to about the Edgartown public pool. She excused herself and stepped into the kitchen.

"Hello, this is Amelia Taylor."

The voice on the other end sent shivers down her spine.

"Amelia. This is Nathan. Nathan Gregory."

Wow. The morning accident was already a distant memory to her.

"Nathan. Hello!" She truly hadn't expected to hear from him like this. She hadn't even had time to pass along news of the accident to her insurance company yet. "Is there something wrong?" she finally asked.

"Wrong? No. Well, I mean, maybe."

"And what's that?"

"Well, see. I found myself at my inn, all ready for a night to myself, and remembered that this is one of my last nights on Martha's Vineyard. I have no one to spend it with."

Amelia's heart jumped into her throat and hammered against her vocal cords.

"I see. That is a tragedy," Amelia said.

"It really is. It makes me ask myself some questions. Like, what the heck am I doing with myself? And others, like, I wonder if that beautiful woman whose morning I ruined wouldn't like to meet at the bar downtown?"

It had been a long, long time since anyone had asked Amelia out on a date. Her first instinct was to say no — that she had family obligations. But Daniel was in for the night; Mandy and Jake didn't need anything from her, so maybe this was her last shot at fun for a bit.

And what the heck? Why not?

"Interesting questions. I wonder if you'll ever find your answers," Amelia teased.

Nathan chuckled. "Come on. Come out with me. I feel awful about this morning. It's really not like me."

"I'm not sure. It's been one crazy day, and I —"

At that moment, Mandy wandered into the kitchen. She listened, furrowed her brow, then mouthed, "Is someone asking you out?"

Amelia shrugged. Embarrassment made her blush slightly as she placed a hand on the counter.

"Go!" Mandy whispered harshly. "Come on!"

"I really think I can make it worth your while," Nathan finally uttered.

Amelia paused for probably way too long. Finally, she replied, "Okay. I can be in Oak Bluffs in twenty minutes."

"Fantastic. There's a bar on Main Street."

"I know the place. See you there."

After Amelia hung up the phone, Mandy smirked and said, "Who was that?"

"Oh, it's um. It's." Amelia ran through her mind for some excuse she could make up. But hadn't she vowed, a long time ago, never to lie to her niece? Another blush rushed over her cheeks as she sighed and said, "It's the guy who hit my car this morning."

Mandy's jaw dropped. "You're kidding."

"Nope."

Mandy disappeared down the shadowy hallway again. Amelia watched, her hand wrapped around her neck. After a long moment, Mandy called, "Aunt Amelia! Aren't you coming?" She then followed after the sound, feeling as though the roles had been reversed. Unfortunately, it was clear: her eighteen-year-old niece had a whole lot more recent experience in this realm than Amelia did. Maybe she really did need her help.

"Here," Mandy said. She passed her a tube of lipstick, some eyeliner, and some mascara. "You work hard—too hard. And all the humidity in the gym made your makeup runoff. You need a retouch."

Amelia stepped toward Mandy's mirror, which she had decorated with photographs of her best friends and various celebrities that Amelia wouldn't have been able to name if her life had depended on it. It was funny how the world took off without you. She hadn't kept up.

"What's this guy's deal?" Mandy asked as Amelia carefully placed eyeliner around her eyes and added a touch of mascara.

"What do you mean?"

"You know. Like, what does he look like? What's his personality?"

Amelia arched an eyebrow and caught Mandy's reflection in the mirror. "He's cute."

"How cute? Like, how can you compare?"

"Do you know who Patrick Dempsey is?"

Mandy's jaw dropped. "No. Way. I'm not too young to know the real McDreamy himself."

"Well, yeah. I would say him, but about fifteen years ago. Forty-ish."

"Wow." Mandy seemed impressed. She crossed and uncrossed her arms, then shifted her head toward the closet. "Do you want to check out my wardrobe?"

Amelia knew that Mandy's closet was a collection of super-tight jeans and super-tight t-shirts, so she respectively declined. Besides, her black dress from her workday wasn't so bad. It was simple; it was almost chic, and she had paid the tiniest bit too much for it when she'd gone out shopping with Mila one day. Traditionally, Mila had the ritziest taste of all of them.

"That lipstick looks perfect on you," Mandy affirmed. "When was the last time you went on a first date, anyway?"

Amelia pondered this. On one hand, she didn't want to reveal such a private thing to her niece; but on the other, Mandy was eighteen and she liked this idea that soon, they would just be close friends, without as much of the pretend-guardian, child relationship.

"I guess it's been like... I don't know. Ten years?" *Had it really been that long?* Suddenly, Amelia's stomach rolled over, and she fell into a state of panic. "Oh my gosh. What am I doing?" she said, mostly to her reflection in the mirror.

"Come on. No way," Mandy said. "I know that look. You won't spiral. Not on my watch."

Amelia stood and walked toward the door. She suddenly fell into a haze. As she went, Mandy reached for her shoulders, held her solidly in place, and made heavy eye contact. Suddenly, Amelia felt much more like one of the younger cheerleaders, receiving a pep talk from their leader.

"Listen to me, Aunt Amelia," Mandy said firmly, locking eyes. "You are beautiful. You are tough. You are actually the most intelligent and wonderful person I've ever had the pleasure of knowing. Your friends love you. The people of Edgartown love you. Disregard any thoughts of fear because all you're doing right now? Is going to see some handsome dude. He's just some dude, but you are Amelia Taylor. And you always will be."

Amelia gave Mandy a soft smile. "Thanks for saying that."

"Of course," Mandy winked. "I might go into public speaking after the whole high school thing."

"Good idea," Amelia replied. "Which reminds me. We should

go back to those college applications. You've only applied to a few. Might as well keep your options open, right?"

"Don't worry about me, right now, Aunt Amelia. That guy is out there and he is waiting for you. Patrick Dempsey, but younger! You said it yourself! Go forth. And get laid."

"Hey!" Amelia blushed at her niece's words. "Don't say that."

Mandy shrugged. "Why not? It's a normal part of life."

Suddenly, Amelia's brother, Daniel, appeared in the hallway. He peered at them curiously. "Nice lipstick," he said. "Are you girls playing dress-up?"

"Yep. Because I'm eight years old, Dad," Mandy smirked.

"Actually, I'm headed out," Amelia said.

"She has a date."

Amelia cast Mandy an ominous look, which forced Mandy to snap her lips together.

"A date?" Daniel echoed his daughter's words. He knew, just as well as everyone else, that Amelia hadn't exactly had time for anyone over the past few years.

"It's just some guy I met this morning," Amelia said. She suppressed a smile and felt that now-familiar blush creep up again. "But it literally doesn't matter."

"He wrecked her car," Mandy added.

"I swear. One more word out of you and you're toast," Amelia said as her smile widened.

Daniel walked Amelia out to her car to inspect the damage. Amelia waved him away as she said, "Danny, you know I can take care of myself, don't you?"

Daniel hadn't bothered with his coat. He crossed his arms, an attempt to keep himself warm against the evening chill. "You take care of everyone else. I should at least try to repay the favor sometimes."

"Don't worry yourself," Amelia told him. "I got this."

"Sure. I know that." Daniel swallowed again, then added, "Thanks for bringing her home tonight. She's a good little actress, but I know she was frightened about it all. It must have been scary to see her fall like that."

"It was," Amelia breathed. "But she's a trooper. She got right back up and clearly improved enough to get me all ready for my not-date. She's as strong as they come."

"As strong as you, maybe," Daniel said. He then tapped the front of her car and added, "Have a good time tonight. You deserve it."

"I don't deserve anything," Amelia said. "And he probably just wants to sue me for driving out in front of his car or something. That's my luck, isn't it?"

CHAPTER FOUR

AMELIA DROVE toward Oak Bluffs in a kind of meditative state. Night had fallen, and just one of her lights shone brightly out across the road. She cursed herself for this; however, she hadn't had a single moment to fix it that afternoon or evening — and now, she was headed right toward the source of the accident. About a block from the bar, she parked and stepped out of her car, just as an icy breeze rushed out from the Vineyard Sound and ruffled her hair. She felt so youthful, so self-conscience in these moments that she very nearly shot back into her car to wipe off the makeup.

But just before she could, she heard her name.

"Amelia!" Nathan Gregory appeared beneath the nearest street lamp and lifted a hand. He looked just as handsome as he had that morning, and his smile was as arrogant as ever.

Amelia's stomach did another little jump as she greeted him. "Hello." Her eyes found his and hunted for a trace of disappointment, which she'd somehow expected to come off of him, as though maybe, he'd remembered her differently. But she found none of that. She found only excitement.

"Thanks for coming all the way over here," Nathan said as they walked across the street toward the bar. "Although it must have been treacherous, with that light broken."

"I'll have it fixed tomorrow," Amelia said.

"Well, let me buy you a drink. Or three," Nathan said, his smile mischievous.

Once they were inside, Nathan and Amelia walked toward a back table, where Nathan asked for her coat. Amelia nearly dropped her purse to the ground as she handed her coat over, proof of how nervous she was. *Could he know that this was her first date in ten years? Could he smell it on her?* Nathan disappeared to hang up their coats, and Amelia studied the bar around her. Toward the far wall, she recognized Lola Sheridan and her boyfriend, Tommy Gasbarro. Lola had her hands pressed over her eyes and her shoulders hunched. Tommy, a rather famous sailor who'd arrived on the island permanently only last year, comforted her. Amelia wasn't sure what was wrong, but she knew better than to stare. She dropped her eyes to the table.

"What can I get you to drink?" Nathan asked as he appeared beside her again.

"Um. Hmm. What about a gin and tonic?"

"Sounds great. I'll have one, too."

Nathan ordered from the bar. Amelia both hated and loved that he kept disappearing, although it only delayed the inevitable. Very soon, they would be engaged in light banter, she hoped. Very soon, she would have to perform the great ritual of "dating." If only

Mandy had read from one of her teenage magazines to give Amelia some tips on how to be smooth and collected.

They clinked glasses and made eye contact. Amelia forced herself to say, "I never imagined I'd get a free G&T out of a little fender-bender."

"Life is a strange thing, isn't it?" Nathan quipped.

"Sure is." Amelia swallowed a gulp of gin and tonic. "So, how do you find Martha's Vineyard so far?"

Nathan shrugged. "I mean, it's not the season for it, is it? March isn't known for its sailing or its beaches. But it's still something special."

"I don't have a favorite season on the Vineyard," Amelia said. "I need all of them. Spring brings growth, and summer brings all the beautiful beach activities, and then autumn is the comedown from summer ..." She paused in the midst of her ramble, suddenly growing embarrassed.

"To everything, there is a season," Nathan said. How was it he seemed to always know what to say?

"A time to live and a time to die," Amelia blurted out. But immediately after she said it, she blushed horribly. *A time to die? What the heck was she rambling about?*

A moment of silence passed between them. Was this what happened on dates? It had been so long that she had no idea.

"But I have pretty good memories here from summers as a kid," Nathan said. He seemed totally at ease with himself, as though whatever came out of his mouth was a-okay with him. "Sailing. Swimming. Flirting with girls."

"Oh! So you're familiar with this place," Amelia replied, swirling the ice in her glass.

"Sure. We came here every summer until I was eighteen or nineteen. I came for a meeting with my father's good friend, an investor who lives between Oak Bluffs and New York."

Amelia nodded, asked relevant questions, and sipped her gin and tonic — admittedly, a bit too quickly. She sucked down the first and then the second and soon found that it was much easier to laugh at Nathan's half-funny jokes. She certainly found it easy to gaze into his cerulean eyes. She imagined herself through the eyes of the other bar-dwellers. Probably they just saw two mature individuals, drinking and flirting. She was on a date, or so she thought. Literally, this was what people did. On purpose. With their time.

She couldn't help but think of about fourteen things on her to-do list that she could have done with this time.

Still, sometimes, she did catch the genuine smile that would stretch across her cheeks every now and then. It was nice to know that someone new found her attractive and interesting and was actually a person outside of work-related issues.

She thought of her sisters — Camilla, Jennifer, Mila, Olivia, and even Michelle. God bless her. Had they seen her out with this guy, they would have been impressed with her boldness. Wasn't it good to just act on a whim? Or was she too old to be acting on impulse?

After the third gin and tonic, Amelia stood up on wobbly legs. She was reminded of baby giraffes, who were birthed into the world and forced immediately to stagger across the land.

"I'll just be a minute," she told Nathan.

She headed into the bathroom to look at her reflection and talk some sense into herself. It had been a long day, one of the longest in recent memory, and there was nothing stopping her from calling a cab and getting herself back to her thousand-count sheets. She'd always slept alone, stretched out in the center of her queen-sized bed and she'd often told herself just how privileged she was to have that life. How often had her friends complained of boyfriends or husbands snoring through the night?

"You did it. You went on a date. Now, go home," she told her reflection. She was reminded of her own mother and hated to admit that sometimes, when she spotted her reflection, she looked a whole lot like her mother, about twenty years before. She'd caught up.

When Amelia stepped out of the bathroom, however, she found Nathan Gregory waiting for her near the door of the bar. His smile was enormous, welcoming, and his eyes glittered wonderfully. He looked at her like she was the only woman in the world. She no longer compared herself to whatever Boston beauty he had back home. She was it, right now in the present.

Suddenly, it felt as though she could fly.

She knew it would happen before it did.

He placed his hand across the small of her back. The alcohol encouraged her to bring her chin upward, brave for whatever came next. Then, she closed her eyes as his lips swept over hers. Suddenly, the world spun around her as she kissed him softly, then with her lips slightly parted. *When was the last time she'd even kissed anyone? It felt like heaven.*

He broke the kiss a few moments later and swept a strand of hair behind her ear. In a whisper, he said, "Can I invite you back to my room for a nightcap?"

Amelia had seen enough movies to know what that meant. She felt yanked in two different directions. On the one hand, she wanted to tell him to call her another night — to do the whole "dating" thing properly. On the other hand, he was headed back to Boston, and she had no idea when he would return.

She nodded. She felt like an innocent young woman, not a forty-year-old. She wasn't a virgin, but she felt like one at the moment.

They walked through the chilly dark night. Silence fell over them until Amelia finally asked, "Where are you staying?"

"The Sunrise Cove. Do you know it?"

Amelia had stayed there years before, when she and Camilla, Mila, Jennifer, and Olivia had decided to pledge their forever allegiance to one another in the wake of Michelle's death. But Amelia didn't want to think about such dark things, not now.

"I do. The Sheridan family has owned it for generations," Amelia said, as though this meant anything to him.

"Huh."

They stepped into the foyer at the Sunrise Cove. A young man sat behind the counter, playing solitaire. The moment he heard them, he snapped to his feet and greeted them with a sleepy smile.

"Good evening, Mr. Gregory," he said. "I hope the bar was an okay recommendation?"

"It really was, Sam," Nathan said. Again, he placed his hand at the base of Amelia's back. "Of course, had a few too many gin and tonics. They really know how to make them there."

"That's the truth. My friend Amanda and I tend to push ourselves a little too far there," Sam said.

Amelia didn't recognize Sam, even as she recognized the name "Amanda Sheridan," who he called his "friend." Perhaps Susan Sheridan had hired new staff members since she'd decided to build back up her criminal defense career. He was certainly handsome. He had that Sheridan glow to him, despite not being related.

"As you should. You're still young," Nathan said with a wink.

He then led Amelia up the stairs to his suite, with its broad bay window that overlooked the Vineyard Sound. The minutes after he clipped the door shut were some of the most anxious of Amelia's life. She no longer remembered herself, or her career, or what people said to one another when they wanted to seem intelligent or beautiful.

But very soon, she realized that none of that mattered. She'd come into a man's room, and she'd done it for one reason and one reason only.

She didn't get much sleep. That's for sure. But as she drifted off, she thanked herself for this one-in-a-million evening. It wasn't like these nights came around for her all the time. Once a decade, if that. She wasn't fully sure if that was pathetic or not. But she did know one thing: her sisters would want to know every detail. And at least, for once, Amelia Taylor was the one with the gossip. What a change.

CHAPTER FIVE

AS AMELIA TAYLOR dressed in yesterday's clothes, her head threatened to explode with the horrors of her gin and tonic hangover. She paired buttons incorrectly, picked at a strange stain on her dress, and furrowed her brow at the reflection in the Sunrise Cove mirror. Was this really the ever-professional, ever-together Amelia Taylor?

The man who'd been her great and mysterious date didn't look so wonderful in the morning, either. He pressed his hands against his forehead and muttered something about a shower. Before she headed out, he dotted a kiss on her cheek and the kiss seemed like a signal. It seemed to say, *"Don't call me. This was nice, but never again."* Amelia wondered if she'd really been that bad or if this was just the ways of the world. One and done.

Ugh. It turned her stomach. As she passed through the hallways of the Sunrise Cove, she prayed that Mandy would find a kind and upstanding man to date and then marry without messing around with all these dating rituals over the next five to ten years. She didn't want Mandy to even touch heartache.

When Amelia appeared in the foyer of the Sunrise Cove, she, of course, nearly stumbled into Susan Sheridan herself. Susan's smile wasn't as electric as it normally was, and her coloring was strange, as though she'd gotten sick again. Of course, Amelia didn't look like herself, either.

"Amelia! I had no idea you were staying with us," Susan said.

Amelia gave a light shrug. "It was a surprise for me as well."

Susan's lips formed a round O. Behind her, Amanda Sheridan wrapped an arm around her cousin, Audrey Sheridan — who, Amelia saw now, was no longer pregnant. She'd had her baby. But there was something about the air between all of them that told Amelia not to say a single word about the baby. Congratulations were clearly not in order.

What had happened?

Amelia excused herself and said, "Have a good day, Susan," then rushed out into the chilly air of the March morning. Her heart thudded with intrigue and sorrow. What on earth had happened with the Sheridan baby? For a long moment, as she staggered back toward the center of Oak Bluffs, she hardly thought of her own sorrows. It was clear: whatever had happened with the Sheridan baby was much, much heavier than a strange one-night stand.

Amelia found her car, just where she'd left it. On the windshield, a parking ticket fluttered. She grumbled inwardly, annoyed with herself for not paying attention to the signs. None of this was like her.

She drove swiftly back to her tiny house at 37 Peases Point Way. She parked in the driveway, hustled inside, and stripped herself bare in the bathroom. The shower stream was razor-sharp and incredibly hot; it was the only thing that drove out some of her thudding headache. Fatigue remained, however, and threatened to destroy her entire day.

As she dressed, she realized for the first time that her phone was dead. How had she forgotten it? Hurriedly, she charged it. A frantic ping-ping-ping told her she'd missed a number of messages, as well —two from her boss, Zane, and one from Mandy.

MANDY: OMG! Tell me everything! How did it go?!

ZANE: We moved the meeting to 8:30. Need you there fifteen minutes before to go over everything.

ZANE: Amelia. Where are you? It's 8:20, and you're late. This isn't like you.

Amelia's stomach dropped. It was now 8:45. According to her schedule, which had basically been tattooed to the back alleys of her mind, she hadn't had a meeting until 10. Zane had clearly altered it late in the night, maybe even as a way to get her into some kind of trouble. Annoyed and panicked, she shot toward the door, her wet hair flung out behind her. In a flurry, she drove toward city hall — daring every car to crash into her. "Make me even later," she growled. "See if I care."

Oh, but she cared. She cared a lot. And when she finally burst into city hall, tears threatened to roll down her cheeks. Her secretary, Clara, hustled up to her, wide-eyed, and stammered, "I tried to call you! Your phone was off! Your phone is never off!"

"I know," Amelia said as she rushed forward without making eye contact. "I just had a late start this morning."

"You never have a late start!" Clara cried. "Zane's in there killing time, but you're the one to speak to about these bigger development issues. You know very well that Zane doesn't have a real grip on many of the laws around here."

Amelia placed her purse on her desk and gave her secretary a crooked smile. "Funny that my boss has no idea what he's doing, isn't it?"

Clara didn't have time to make jokes. All the color had drained from her cheeks. "The developer is angry. I heard him demanding why he couldn't begin his presentation yet. Another one of these big-whig, super-rich city types."

"Another? I really think we should kick them off the island," Amelia grumbled. Somehow, the idea that Zane was currently panicked had calmed her nerves. She glanced into the mirror near her desk and saw a woman with nearly-perfect makeup, slight bags under her eyes, and wet hair. "I think I need to improvise," she told both her secretary and her reflection. Hurriedly, she grabbed a scarf and wrapped it around the top of her forehead, then allowed her dark curls to spill down. Some of them had dried into coils.

"Not half bad," Clara said, clearly surprised. "It's not your typical look, but I guess it will have to do."

Amelia gathered her notes, lifted her chin, and marched toward the boardroom. As she stepped in, she spotted Zane in conversation with yet another ritzy-looking, handsome city-guy. How tired she was of these guys, especially after her night with Nathan.

"Ah! Here she is." Zane's eyes tore over her slightly-different hair as he stood. "Oliver, this is Amelia Taylor. She's a force of nature around here. Amelia, this is Oliver Krispin."

Amelia placed her notepad and folders on the mahogany table and stretched her hand across the space between them. "Oliver. Lovely to meet you."

"You as well." His eyes were bright green, and his smile was sure yet difficult to read. Probably, he wasn't so pleased that she'd made him wait a full half-hour and she'd arrived a half-mess.

"Apologies for my tardiness," Amelia said as she sat across from him. "I had some technological difficulties, and I didn't receive the news that the meeting time had been changed in time."

"Technological difficulties! In this day and age?" Oliver said with a laugh.

"I know. Hard to believe," Amelia said. Her nostrils flared with anger. Why couldn't he just take her excuse and let it go? He was just like Nathan. Just another guy, prepared to take advantage of her or belittle her, armed with his money and his self-assurance.

"I just hope it isn't the kind of thing I have to get used to here on Martha's Vineyard," Oliver said. "I have to keep a pretty strict schedule since I'm so often between here and New York."

"Of course you are," Amelia said. There was just the slightest disdain to her voice; she couldn't fully cover it up. "And let's not waste any more of your time now. I would love to hear more about your project. We just love when creative minds come to our island and broaden our horizons."

Had one of her girls heard that last sentence, they might have burst into laughter. It reeked of sarcasm. Of course, neither Oliver nor Zane sensed it. *This was the way of men sometimes, wasn't it? Why had she gone on that date again?*

"Very well then," Oliver said. He was clearly ready to take any compliment. He stood, clicked a button, and then, his presentation appeared in light on the wall beside him. "My pitch to you today encapsulates the height of boutique hotels, spas, resorts, and all that Martha's Vineyard tourists flock here in the summertime for. But my resort? It broadens on what you already do well here, and it sets itself up for some of the highest rollers this island has ever seen. I know already, this previous Thanksgiving, Martha's Vineyard played host to one of the most expensive weddings of the century. I'm talking about that level of money coming into the island all the time. That's what this resort would do for you and the people of Edgartown and all of Martha's Vineyard."

That whole thing, with Charlotte Hamner planning a wedding in about three weeks for a famous actress — it had annoyed Amelia a great deal, as she'd had to help with a number of the permits and such. It had been a headache. Of course, that level of money coming into the island was nothing to scoff at, especially in front of Zane, who cared about that sort of thing above all else.

"Very intriguing," Zane said now as he tapped a finger on his chin.

"I thought so, too," Oliver said, clearly pleased with himself. "Shall I outline some of the major elements of the resort for you now?"

"Absolutely," Zane nodded.

"Hold on just a moment." Amelia held up a finger. Annoyance flooded her heart and took hold of her tongue.

"Yes?"

"I think it's necessary that we discuss the various permits and such that you'll need prior to breaking ground on this establishment," she said. She made heavy eye contact with Oliver as if to say, *Don't mess with me. I'm in charge here.*

"I see. Permits," Oliver acknowledged.

"You'll need to make sure you get an environmentalist crew out there to approve that you aren't messing up any important ecosystems. We here on Martha's Vineyard care a great deal about the nature around us—including all birds and other animals that live on the island alongside us."

Oliver looked at her like she was nuts. She had, in fact, just compared people to birds — but she was prepared to do it again.

"Beyond these various environmentalist permits, you'll need a building permit, a plumbing permit, an electrical permit, and a mechanical permit. You'll also need to present your plans in front of the tourism management group here to ensure it aligns with our vision for Martha's Vineyard."

"I kind of thought that's what this meeting was." Oliver arched a brow.

Amelia chuckled unkindly. "I'm afraid it's not totally up to me, although I do belong to the tourism management group."

"Of course you do," Oliver said, his voice smooth and cultured.

"Let's not get ahead of ourselves, Amelia," Zane jumped in. His eyes flashed angrily. "Oliver has hardly told us a single thing about his resort plan, and already, you're stretching out all this red tape."

"I feel like I've been arrested," Oliver said to Zane.

The two of them laughed together. Amelia had been in settings like this before: where men liked to think they were above her, belittle her, display a little chauvinism. But everything she'd said was true. Oliver really did have to jump through these hoops if he wanted to build his ritzy resort.

"I'm sorry. I guess I don't get the joke," Amelia said.

"She never does," Zane told Oliver.

Again, they laughed. Annoyed, exhausted, and overwhelmed, Amelia stood from the table and collected her things. "I'm terribly sorry. I have another meeting scheduled after this one, and I don't have time for theatrics or rudeness. If you'd like to have a professional meeting about your plans and how you hope to get these relevant permits, then we can reschedule something in the near future. If you do decide to change the time, last-minute, let me know as soon as possible."

"Will do," Oliver said. His voice was hard-edged. "As long as you have enough time to do your hair, we should be good."

Amelia paused in the doorway, yanked her head around, and glared at him. Gosh, he looked pleased with himself. Probably, the thought of an imperfect woman turned his stomach, especially him being a New Yorker and all.

"I didn't realize the nature of my hair had any effect on your presentation, Mr. Krispin. How awful for you."

Amelia then disappeared through the door and marched back to her office. Once at her desk, she collapsed and placed her forehead on the wood. What she felt now was very strange — a mix of triumph and total, all-encompassing anger and shame.

CHAPTER SIX

IT WAS a day that would forever live in infamy as one of the most annoying of Amelia's life. Each meeting seemed to drift forward, second-after-second, so that she questioned the very nature of time itself. Just after one-thirty, she told her secretary she couldn't hack it anymore — that she needed to reschedule all her meetings for the rest of the week. Her secretary looked at her like she had three heads.

"I just don't feel like myself," Amelia said. "And I don't want to screw anything else up."

This was putting it lightly.

Amelia returned home, changed into a pair of jeans and a sweatshirt, and sat on the floor by the couch. She stared at the wall for a number of minutes. Memories from the night before sizzled in the back of her mind. Rage toward Nathan, toward Oliver, toward all men for their arrogance and their lack of love for her, spun through her. Mostly, though, she hated that she'd allowed herself to feel anything for anyone, especially when she had known that anything with Nathan was short-term, or even less than that—a fling and nothing more.

Women like her had flings. It wasn't this crazy, out-of-the-box thing. Why, then, did she feel so crazy?

Just past three, Amelia called Olivia. The bell had just rung at the high school, and through the phone, Amelia could hear the frantic cries from the high school hallway.

"Amelia! Hey! I was just wrapping up here and prepping to head over to the mansion."

"Ah. Another day of hard labor ahead of you?"

"Something like that," Olivia replied. She had inherited an old, historic mansion from her great aunt and had spent the majority of the past few months fixing it up. Since then, she'd also fallen in love with the man her great aunt had hired to build it back up. In Amelia's eyes, it was as though Great Aunt Marcia had known all along Olivia might find love with Anthony.

"Gotcha. Well, that's okay. I was just curious if you could talk."

"Of course! Why don't you come over to the house? You can talk while I spackle. It's boring work, anyway." Olivia paused for a moment and then said, "It's a little early for you to be out of work, isn't it?"

"I left a little early."

"Sometimes, you're there till nine at night."

"Okay, so I left a lot early," Amelia quipped. "But I had to get out of there."

Olivia's voice shifted to reflect her worry. "You'll explain when you get there?"

"Sure. Yeah. Okay."

Amelia drove the familiar route out toward the old historic building and parked to the left of Anthony's big truck. When she appeared at the door, Olivia hollered through the second-floor window. "Let yourself in and come on up!"

Anthony and Olivia were both on the second floor, working in separate rooms. Anthony waved a sturdy hand from down the hall and said, "Good to see you, Amelia!"

"You too!" Amelia replied as she swept past and entered the bedroom toward the right side of the hallway, where Olivia stood to tackle her spackling task. She looked giddy, like a much younger girl, and she grinned madly at Amelia with her little metal tool lifted toward the wall.

"Welcome back to our chaos," Olivia said. "I won't put you to work this time." She then furrowed her brow and added, "You look a bit..."

"Exhausted? Hungover?" Amelia finished. "I'm all of those things and more."

Olivia's eyes bugged out. "You got drunk on a work night?"

"I know. It's not like me," Amelia said. She then chewed at her lower lip, turned her eyes toward the ground, and admitted it. "I had a — um — one-night stand."

Olivia dropped the metal spackling tool. It rattled around on the ground as she gaped. "You're joking."

"I'm not," Amelia said. Her heart thudded somberly. "I wish I was."

Olivia rushed toward her, fell to her knees, and gripped Amelia's shoulders. "Oh, my God! This is huge!" Her voice was laced with excitement.

"Is it? Because I feel crazy."

"It's huge. I promise," Olivia said. "I mean, when was the last time you ... Well, not that I can talk. Before I met Anthony, well." she shrugged. They knew each other's history like the backs of their own hands. "But it doesn't sound like it was the best of times?"

Amelia shrugged. "He was handsome and sometimes funny. And very rich. And sure, it was fine and fun and a life experience. But then I was late to this meeting this morning, and I kind of made a fool of myself. And don't get me started on what it feels like to do a walk of shame at the age of forty."

Olivia buzzed her lips. "Listen, Amelia. Over the past decade, you've worked yourself to death. You've hardly given a moment to yourself. So what? You had a walk of shame? That's incredible! You got yourself out of your normal, everyday schedule, and you experienced something new!"

Amelia scrunched her nose. She played with a strand of hair, which had now morphed into a strange curly mass since she hadn't been able to monitor it properly since it had dried. "I look like a muppet," she confessed.

Olivia burst into laughter. "You're way too hard on yourself. I know that's the Amelia way."

A tear trickled out of the side of Amelia's eye. She placed her finger against it to catch it and then lifted her tear up into the light. "I can't believe I shed a single tear over Nathan Gregory."

"The tear doesn't have to be for him," Olivia told her. "It can be a tear for how beautiful it is to meet and connect with a stranger and then, maybe, never see him again. But for a moment, you two were everything to one another."

"You really do have a poetic way of looking at things," Amelia said, her voice doubtful.

"I have to. I teach creative writing," Olivia said teasingly.

A few hours later, Amelia collected herself up, wrapped her emotions uptight, and said goodbye to Olivia. "I told Jake I'd go to his basketball game."

"Cheerleading one night, basketball the next," Olivia said. "You're busier than most moms."

"You know I can't miss these things," Amelia said.

"Those kids are so lucky to have you," Olivia offered. "I just hope you don't run yourself too ragged. I'm sure you can miss a game here and there."

Amelia chuckled. "No. I really can't." Not with Suzy so far away. Amelia had made a promise to her brother — to be there for his children in every single capacity. She wasn't the kind to break her promises.

AMELIA MET her brother and her parents at the high school gymnasium. She'd hardly eaten a thing over the course of the day, and she was grateful when her father appeared beside her with an extra hot dog, with extra relish, just like she liked it. Jason and Anita Taylor, her lovely and loving parents, had worked together as architects throughout their careers until they'd ultimately retired a few years before. Her father gave her a strange look as she accepted the hot dog, as though he could see directly through to her strange day of pain.

"How are you doing, Ames?"

Amelia tried on a fake smile. "Not so bad. And yourself?"

"I'm prepared for another wild night of high school sports!" he replied.

"Good to hear," Amelia said as she made eye contact with her mother. "How was your day, Mom?"

"I've decided to totally change the kitchen," her mother announced. "I'm drawing up plans as we speak."

Amelia laughed. "You really couldn't stay retired, could you?"

"As if you could ever stop working, Amelia," her mother said with a sneaky smile. "You're just as addicted as we are."

"I guess so," Amelia said. And in truth, she was grateful that she had gotten such a stellar work ethic from her parents. They were lucky to enjoy the fields they'd chosen. Even Daniel gave so much of himself to his museum work.

Together, they sat near the middle section of the bleachers. Daniel smacked his palms together and focused, watching as his son warmed up, bobbing and weaving through the other players as his jersey swept out behind him. He was a thin kid with wiry muscles, and his face looked like someone else's — not the normal Jake they were accustomed to back at the house. He was in sport-mode.

"I heard you were here for poor Mandy's fall last night," her mother said as she furrowed her brow. "I can't imagine. It just terrifies me to think of it."

"It was scary," Amelia affirmed. "But she popped right back up after a while. She's resilient, that girl."

"She gets a lot of that from her aunt." Anita winked. "Oh, you know, I heard something awful today."

Amelia arched her brow. Had news of her one-night stand reached her mother's ears? She supposed it wouldn't have surprised her. After all, she had been spotted several times at the Sunrise Cove, and news traveled fast on the island.

"You've heard about that pregnant Sheridan girl. Audrey," Anita continued.

"Yes." In fact, Amelia had seen the poor girl earlier that morning — no longer pregnant, with a face paler than the moon.

"Well, she gave birth. Late February, I think. And the poor baby is quite sick. They've kept him in the NICU ever since."

Amelia's heart dropped. "That's just awful."

"It really is. The girl had a surprise pregnancy. She was meant to be off to Penn State for her sophomore year in journalism. Now, she's facing some of the biggest hardships of her life. It's a good thing that the Sheridan family is so strong. She has a good support network."

"Yes. True."

The basketball players lined up as the announcer read off their names. Amelia smacked her palms together loudly, then even louder for her nephew, Jake Taylor. He beamed at the stands, at his father and his aunt and his grandparents, and then hustled back to the bench to prep for the first few minutes of the game.

The cheerleaders arranged themselves toward the far end of the basketball court, beneath the basketball hoop. Amelia found Mandy toward the back of the other cheerleaders, which wasn't customary. Normally, she liked to be front and center.

But there seemed to be something off about Mandy, now. She couldn't fully use her hurt shoulder, yet it seemed like, although she performed all the motions with her good arm and jumped around just as high as the others. But it was her face that told Amelia another story. Her eyes were sorrowful; her hair wasn't as curly and vibrant, and between various scored points of the game, Mandy looked on the verge of tears.

It was such a direct reflection of what Amelia felt. It was as though Mandy had bottled up all of Amelia's disappointments, fears and sadness from the previous twenty-four hours. Maybe she was just upset about the cheerleading competition? She had put a lot of effort into it.

At half-time, Edgartown High School was a full ten points ahead of Falmouth. Daniel was wild with excitement. "I'm going to the concession stand. Does anyone need anything? Popcorn? A soda?"

Anita and Jason both ordered diet cokes, while Amelia said she didn't need anything. When Daniel disappeared up the steps, Amelia spotted Mandy yet again in the corner of the gym. She had her hands over her eyes, and her shoulders shook — as though she was in pain. Beside her, a friend whispered in her ear.

Maybe it was a boy? A broken heart? A bad test score? Just PMS? It really could have been anything.

Amelia held herself back. It did nobody any good for her to make a scene now, in front of much of the school and all their parents. She remembered her teenage years well and knew that back then, she'd really only needed her girls, Camilla, Michelle, Jennifer, Mila and Olivia, by her side. Still, she made a mental note to take Mandy out for a lunch date soon. She needed a woman in her life she could depend on, whether she knew she did or not, Aunt Amelia wasn't about to let her down.

CHAPTER SEVEN

IT TOOK a few days for Amelia to shake herself free of the icky feeling of her one-night stand. Sure, Olivia, Camilla, Jennifer, and Mila sent her a number of "you go, girl" texts, which pepped her up and it wasn't like work wasn't as full-on as ever. By the time Friday night came around, Amelia had found herself no longer checking her phone as often, just in case Nathan Gregory had decided to send her a "Hey, we should do this again" text. She knew better than to expect that, anyway. He wasn't the type, and he'd probably already had a few other, similar nights with other women back in Boston.

Probably, those women knew how to have actual, human conversations over drinks. Amelia couldn't help but play out some of the things she'd said to him and wince.

Friday evening, Jennifer stopped by Peases Point Way for some pizza. They wore sweat pants and dove into some big Edgartown Pizza pie, stretching the gooey cheese up with each slice and eating about two slices too many. Jennifer spoke about her romance and now full-on relationship with Derek, and Amelia was again reminded of the first days Jennifer had ever crushed on Joel, her ex-husband. It was wonderful to see her so vibrant again, like a little kid.

"What did it feel like to be back on a date?" Jennifer asked, after a small silence.

Amelia chewed her lower lip. "It felt awkward. Horrible. Like I had three heads."

Jennifer chuckled. "I guess I understand that."

"It didn't make me want to run out and find another person to date if that's what you want to know," Amelia said, picking off an olive and popping it into her mouth.

"I'm not pestering you," Jennifer said, although her eyes glittered, as though Amelia had hurt her. "I just care about you. And I know you have a lot of love to give."

Amelia collected the plates and walked toward the kitchen, where she placed them at the bottom of the sink. It had always been apparent that her sisters thought she lived a smaller, less-than existence, as she had never been in love or had children.

Jennifer followed her into the kitchen, seemingly prepared to apologize. But Amelia just waved her hand, proof it wasn't necessary. As Jennifer searched out the ice cream in the freezer, Amelia texted Mandy. She hadn't heard from her since the day of the basketball game, which wasn't like her. Even when Amelia had texted to say her date had been "kind of a dud," Mandy hadn't followed up. Mandy, at eighteen years old, was one of the nosiest people Amelia knew. Something was amiss.

AMELIA: Mandy! Hey! Do you have plans for lunch tomorrow?

Mandy texted back almost immediately. This was confusing, also. A popular cheerleader wasn't the kind of girl to be stuck at home on a Friday, checking her text messages.

MANDY: Nope.

This one-word response also turned Amelia's stomach. Normally, Mandy texted her with non-stop heart emojis and exclamation marks.

AMELIA: Want to meet at Nancy's? Around one?

Jennifer placed the carton of ice cream on the counter. "You look worried."

Amelia chuckled. "That's just what my face looks like. I need a facial from Mila, stat."

"Come on, Amelia. You'd tell me if something was really off, right? This guy from Boston, he's just a typical player. Think of it as a fun time. Nothing more. You're absolutely entitled to one and to not feel ashamed afterward. He should consider himself lucky."

"I know. But we aren't used to that, are we? That type of thing."

Jennifer shook her head. "To be honest, I think that kind of thing might have destroyed me, too."

Jennifer spooned them up bowls of French Vanilla ice cream as Mandy texted back.

MANDY: Sure. See you there.

THE FOLLOWING AFTERNOON, Amelia donned a cream-colored dress and a thicker jean jacket, along with a pair of brown boots and some of her trendiest jewelry. It was a Saturday, which meant nobody expected the "business Amelia" and she liked to show off her more fashionable side to Mandy. Somehow, it was proof that she still cared, that she remained youthful and that she hadn't yet given up even though it seemed increasingly clear that she would never find Mr. Right.

Mandy was a full fifteen minutes late. Again, this wasn't entirely like her, although Amelia would let it slide. Amelia sipped her ice water and gazed out at the magnificent view of the Nantucket Sound, at the way the early springtime light played out across the waves. How lucky they were to have this island. How lucky they were to live in the midst of this gorgeous, natural environment surrounded by some of the most loving humans on the planet.

People like Nathan Gregory and that other developer, Oliver Krispin, didn't belong.

"Hey, Aunt Amelia." Mandy appeared next to the table. She wore a simple, loose-fitting black dress, and her eyes were somber and lined with more charcoal than normal.

Amelia jumped to her feet to hug her. Mandy hardly lifted her arms.

"How does your shoulder feel?" Amelia asked as Mandy gathered herself across the table and opened the menu.

"Hmm? Oh. It's fine. It pinches from time to time, but nothing major."

"It's crazy how flexible you are," Amelia noted, stealing a glance at her niece. "If anyone else had taken that tumble, they would have shattered into a million pieces."

"Hmm."

Mandy had never given off such an aura of coldness. Even as she'd grown beautiful and popular at school, she had always been a welcoming ball of energy to Amelia.

The server arrived to take their orders. Amelia ordered a crab salad, while Mandy went with a lobster bisque. They also ordered rolls for the table. Mandy passed over her menu and then turned her eyes out toward the water. It was really profound how beautiful she was. She looked a lot like her mother, Suzy, although Amelia never brought that up.

"I should tell you more about my date the other night," Amelia said suddenly. Maybe this was how she could connect with her?

"Oh. Right."

"He was so full of himself," Amelia started. "Very handsome, successful and very used to the whole dating thing. I felt like a fish out of water."

Mandy nodded somberly. "At least you looked really hot when you left our house."

Amelia felt a blush creep up her neck. "Thanks for saying that. Actually, it helps a lot."

"Men only really care about that, anyway," Mandy said. "So, if you said something dumb or whatever, he isn't thinking about that."

Amelia furrowed her brow. "Some men really do care about other things, Mandy."

"Oh? Have you found one who does?"

The silence stretched between them as the waiter arrived to place the basket of rolls between them. Neither of them touched the bread, even as the salty fragrance steamed over them. Amelia wanted to reference Jennifer's ex-husband, Joel, or the newly-found Anthony, or even Mila's husband, now-deceased, Peter. But she had no real experience of her own, and it felt dishonest.

"That's what I thought," Mandy said.

Lunch continued on like this for the next forty-five minutes. Each time Amelia tried to bring up a topic they normally discussed like cheerleading, or Mandy's plans for after graduation, or Mandy's best friends, or even, heck, whatever had gone on in the world of pop culture the previous week — Mandy brushed it off, shrugged her shoulders, or made some kind of sour comment.

Generally, her mood was: *don't push me. I'm about to burst.*

Mandy moved her food around her plate with her fork and then placed it to the side when she'd eaten a few morsels. Her skin looked pale, almost green. Amelia gestured for the server to come with the bill, and she paid hurriedly as they sat together in silence. She'd read many "mother of teenager" blogs about this kind of topic, but she'd hardly ever seen Mandy like this. She felt like a boat without an anchor.

"Do you want to go for a walk along the water?" Amelia heard herself ask. She hated that she sounded like a nervous mother.

Mandy shrugged, but donned her coat, crossed her arms over her chest, and followed Amelia out into the sun. Amelia placed her hand at the top of Mandy's back as they turned toward the docks. A breeze tilted the sailboats to-and-fro so that the sterns creaked against the boards of the docks.

"It's a beautiful day, isn't it?" Amelia asked.

Mandy just cleared her throat. Amelia sensed that she wanted to make some kind of excuse and get out of there, but for whatever reason, Mandy remained by her side, still unspeaking. Amelia searched through the back alleys of her mind for some kind of topic —anything.

"That guy, you know, he took me to the Sunrise Cove," Amelia said. "I don't think I've slept outside of my house with a guy in... well. It's been a very long time. But I'm terrified the whole island will be up in arms about it sooner than later. The Sheridans definitely spotted me."

"Hmm," Mandy offered.

"But I guess they have a lot more to worry about right now," Amelia continued. Her cheeks burned. "Audrey had her baby, and he's apparently very sick. I'm sure they hardly saw me when I walked through the foyer."

Mandy stopped dead on the sidewalk. Amelia bustled ahead for a moment until she realized Mandy had faltered. She turned back, expecting Mandy to be tying her shoe or something. But instead, Mandy just stood there, her eyes bugged out and her shoulders quivering.

"What's wrong, honey?" Amelia demanded. She could hear the worry, heavy in her voice. She was done pretending.

Mandy's upper teeth cut over her lower lip as though she tried to strain against her sobs.

"Mandy. Mandy, honey, do you want to sit down?"

Amelia led Mandy toward the nearest bench. Together, they perched at the edge of it. Mandy's eyes tore out toward the far horizon, while Amelia kept her eyes on Mandy's. There was definitely something up.

"I wish you would tell me what's going on," Amelia murmured

softly. "I told you a long time ago. I'm here for you, no matter what. Remember?"

The first tear rolled down Mandy's cheek. It reflected the light of the sun.

"I didn't mean to do it," she finally whispered.

Amelia's mind spun to countless options — *a failed test? A fight with another student? What?*

Mandy pressed her fingers against her eyes and exhaled. "I know what you're going to say. You're going to say you went to all that trouble to talk to me about it for nothing. You're going to say —"

"Hey. Don't put words in my mouth," Amelia said. Her words were gentle yet firm. "Just tell me what's going on. And we can figure it out together."

Mandy dropped her fingers to reveal red-tinged eyes. After a long, horrible stretch of silence, she finally said, "I'm pregnant."

Amelia's heart sank, albeit just the slightest bit. She reached forward, gripped both of Mandy's hands, and didn't allow an extra second of emptiness to pass. Mandy let out the first of what would be many sobs.

"Hey. Hey, Mandy. It's okay." Amelia placed her hand on Mandy's hair and brought the girl's head against her shoulder. "Mandy, really."

"I'm so sorry. I let you down. I let everyone down." Mandy's voice was hardly heard beyond her cries. "And now, I have no idea what to do. I can't tell Dad. He'll kill me. And oh my, God, what about college? I haven't even picked a school. I —"

But Amelia pressed her hand a bit harder on the girl's forehead.

"Shhh," she exhaled. "Mandy, listen to me. Listen. For just a minute, okay?"

Slowly, Mandy calmed herself just enough so that she could hear.

"When your dad found out your mom was pregnant with you, he came to my office. He was white as a sheet. I thought he was going to faint. He told me he wasn't sure if he was ready. He told me he'd always wanted to be a father but that he had never actually seen himself in the role. He was afraid he would mess everything up.

"But now, look at him, Mandy. Look at your dad. You'd never know that, would you? When you were born, he carried you around so proudly. He took to it like that." She snapped her fingers. "And every single moment since you first came into this world, he's been your dad first, and everything else second."

Mandy blinked her big, beautiful, tear-filled eyes. "What do you mean?"

"I mean that you'll be the same. You'll step up to the plate. You'll feel more love for this baby than you even knew you had in you. And this moment, here on the docks right now? This moment of fear? It will feel like a distant memory."

"I hope you're right, Aunt Amelia," Mandy murmured softly. "I really do."

CHAPTER EIGHT

"JUST ANOTHER MANIC MONDAY," Amelia breathed as she tossed her head back, gripped the steering wheel, and eased herself back toward city hall. It had been a trying weekend, to say the least, and now it had vomited her up on yet another Monday morning, somehow a full week after her dramatic accident and one-night stand. With a funny jolt in her gut, she realized she still hadn't had her front light fixed. There had simply been too much going on.

Throughout the weekend, Mandy had pleaded with Amelia to give her a few more weeks to think before they told her father the news. Amelia had to respect her wishes, although she hated hiding this news from her brother. The previous evening, as they'd all gathered for pizza and movies, Daniel had again thanked her for all her efforts in the "mom department" as they had stood in the kitchen together alone. She'd blushed and wondered if this was a kind of betrayal.

But she couldn't betray Mandy, above all. It was her body. It was her baby.

When Amelia arrived at city hall, she greeted her secretary warmly and added, "Great that I'm not late, huh? Considering I was late twice last week. Pretty good record."

"Actually, Ms. Taylor, you should know..." Clara began, just as Amelia pushed open her office door.

There, seated across from her normal chair, was Oliver Krispin. Amelia's heart jumped into her throat, and her mind spun with a strange mix of anger and then intrigue. In all her years, nobody had just come into her office without an appointment. It took a great amount of confidence. Or, in the case of Oliver Krispin, a good deal of arrogance and a lack of respect for other people's time and space.

"Mr. Krispin. What a surprise," Amelia said as she flared her nostrils.

Oliver stood and unbuttoned his suit jacket as though he wanted to show off the clearly expensive buttons and the gorgeous stitching on the pockets. Amelia was a sucker for fine details, although it wasn't like she'd announce that to him just then. In fact, she would never compliment Oliver Krispin or men like him — ever.

"Good morning, Ms. Taylor. Your secretary mentioned that you have a busy schedule today, so I took the liberty of ensuring I could catch you beforehand."

Amelia's heels clacked around the side of the desk. She removed her coat and shook her head the slightest bit so that her curls erupted down her shoulders. If she wasn't mistaken, Oliver caught every motion of her hips, her hair, and her shoulders.

Good. Maybe she wanted him to check her out, just the slightest bit before she crushed him.

"And what do you think you'd do, Mr. Krispin, had I broken into your office before your jam-packed schedule ahead?" Amelia asked.

Oliver's eyes glittered. He placed a folder on the desk before her and gestured. "You can find all the relevant paperwork right in this file. All the permits. Everything. I want to be able to break ground on the project by the end of March."

"So you decided to ignore my question?" Amelia asked with a hearty laugh. "Bold."

"Think of it this way, Amelia," Oliver said. "That is if I can call you Amelia."

"You cannot."

"Well, then, Ms. Taylor. Think of it this way. If you look at those permits and approve me right now, then the two of us won't have to see one another very much moving forward. You can go on with all your bland Edgartown rituals, and I can break ground on something truly profound, something that will revolutionize the clientele of Martha's Vineyard over the next few years."

"You say that as though we have a bad reputation," Amelia said haughtily. "And we don't."

"Of course you don't," Oliver reassured her. "I wish only to add to that. To make it flourish."

Amelia detested this man. She hated the vibrant spark of his green eyes, and the way he wore his suit, and the confident, beautiful smile across his lips. But he was right: if she approved his permits now, they could step out of one another's way, and she would have more time to devote to the island and the people she cared about the most.

"I'll look over your permits," Amelia said somberly. "But I don't have long. And if there's anything the slightest bit out of order, know that you'll have to re-do it and set up a formal meeting with me later on, at a time that I agree to. Is that clear?"

"Crystal," Oliver replied, his nostrils flared.

Amelia sat at the edge of her desk chair and began to read over the various permits and documents. Throughout, Oliver placed his right foot over his left knee and seemed hyper-focused on her. Occasionally, Amelia glanced up to catch those big, earnest green eyes, full-on glaring at her. It was almost like he wanted to intimidate her until she agreed to let him go.

Much of the paperwork was exactly correct. In fact, Amelia marveled that he'd gotten so much of it correct.

But as she neared the final end of the stack, her heart thudded with excitement.

He had really thought he'd gotten away with something. He had really thought she wouldn't notice, what with all the other papers to inspect.

Slowly, she lifted her chin and closed the folder. She couldn't help it: she smirked at him.

"Mr. Krispin, I regret to inform you that you're missing a very important document."

Oliver arched his brow. "Everything's in there. Everything you told me you needed."

"That's not true," she corrected him. "And the fact that you didn't think I would notice is something of an insult to me."

"I haven't tried to get anything past you," Oliver scoffed.

"And yet, you've completely left out the paper that explains where exactly you plan to build. It states here in your introduction paragraph that you wish to build on the land on the southern edge of the island. Much of that area is both historic and preserved, which means the where of it all is much more important."

Oliver leaned forward ominously. He placed his hands beneath his chin and clucked his tongue.

"I see you're beginning to remember that you forgot that very important document, aren't you?" Amelia said with the slightest hint of sarcasm. "How dreadful. I guess you won't be able to start that late-March build, after all."

"The money this development would bring to your island is astronomical," Oliver replied, his voice low. "You would really give up on that? For a bit of preserved land? Look around this place! There's preserved land everywhere you look!"

Amelia snapped the folder on the desk. "You know why it's all around us? Because people like me protect it from men like you. That's why."

Oliver stood in a huff. His cheeks were blotchy. He reached for the folder of papers, but before he could grip them, Amelia tossed them in the trash. He balked at her as she crossed her arms over her chest.

"You'll have to start all over, I'm afraid," she informed. "What a shame."

Oliver buttoned and unbuttoned his suit jacket. "You'll really regret this, Ms. Taylor."

"I'm honestly pretty sure I won't, Mr. Krispin," Amelia snapped back. "Now, would you kindly excuse yourself from my office? As you've already mentioned, I have a number of things to take care of. And none of those things has anything at all to do with that ritzy development you crave. You know, the one that will probably never exist."

Amelia watched this deflated man stomp out of her office and then slammed the door closed behind him. Amelia grinned inwardly and began to scribble various notes for the day ahead in her day planner. When she glanced back up, her secretary stood in the doorway, wide-eyed.

"What the heck did you do to that guy?" she asked.

Amelia shrugged. "I told him the rules. I don't think he's the kind of guy who's ever heard the rules before."

With that, she returned to her schedule ahead, grateful that she'd had the gumption to tell that guy what she really felt. She needed to do that more in her life. Perhaps this was day one.

CHAPTER NINE

THE NEXT FEW days flew past in a kind of a blur. Yet again, Amelia juggled multiple meetings, Jake's basketball games, calls from her sisters, along with multiple panicked text messages from Mandy, who seemed to need constant affirmation that Amelia wasn't going to up and tattle on Mandy for being pregnant. Amelia understood this, yet also felt the conversation with Daniel coming like a dark storm. One day soon, they would have to face the consequences of what had happened.

Mid-way through March, Amelia headed out of the grocery store and nearly stumbled head-first into Susan Sheridan herself. Unlike the previous time Amelia had seen her, Susan looked much brighter, and her smile was immediate.

"Amelia!" she said. "What a surprise. What brings you over to Oak Bluffs?"

"I just had a business meeting, actually," Amelia said. Her heart hammered with intrigue. She wanted so desperately to ask about the health of Baby Sheridan. "It's such a beautiful day out here. I almost want to walk back to Edgartown."

Susan laughed. "I know exactly what you mean." She stepped back out onto the sidewalk with Amelia and lifted her cheeks toward the sun. "Gosh, it's been a strange year so far."

Amelia shifted her weight. "For us over in Edgartown, too."

"I'm sure. You know, I'd been away from the Vineyard for about twenty-five years. I had made up my mind about the place. I told myself it was just this sleepy island where nothing happened. But since then, wow. I had cancer. I've gotten engaged. I've made peace with my sisters, who I love so deeply. And my daughter has moved to the Vineyard, at least for now, and gone through heartache of her own."

"That's enough to fill at least a few memoirs," Amelia said.

"You're telling me. When Audrey had her baby and he was so sick, I thought maybe all our good luck had dried up. But he's finally home! I can't believe it. He's adorable, Amelia."

Amelia's heart lifted. She remembered that when she'd told Mandy about Audrey's sick baby, Mandy's face had twisted with fear and horror, and she'd burst into tears.

"That's such good news." Amelia's voice caught in her throat. "Give Audrey and everyone else my best. What's his name?"

"Max," Susan said, beaming with excitement. "Another generation of Sheridans on Martha's Vineyard. It just blows me away."

As Amelia walked back to her car, she thought about Mandy's baby, about Audrey's baby and about how this next generation would see countless Martha's Vineyard summers, would hike the hills at Felix Neck and dive into the salty waters. It had been a long time since Amelia had given up all hope on her own children, but knowing that she would be there for Mandy's baby, for his or her first smile and first steps, pleased her more than she could say. It filled her heart with joy.

When she got back in her car, she called Mandy, who answered almost immediately.

"Hey! I'm so glad you answered," Amelia said.

"I skipped cheerleading. What's the point?" Mandy said softly.

Amelia scrunched her nose as she eased her car out into the brewing traffic of a late afternoon. "I can understand that." It was true. She really could. "I wanted to tell you something. Something pretty good, actually."

"I could use some good news, I guess."

"Remember how I told you about Audrey Sheridan's baby? Well, he's better now. He's doing so well that he's now home with his family."

Mandy was silent for a long time. Amelia pressed her foot against the brake and blinked through the glass, up at the stoplight. She couldn't breathe.

Finally, Mandy let out a sob. "I don't know if it's the pregnancy hormones or what. But this is one of the best things I've ever heard. I'm just so glad."

FRIDAY EVENING, the front buzzer of Amelia's place at Peases Point Way rang. She zipped up her sweatshirt and scrambled to answer it. There, with three massive pizza boxes in his arms, stood the traditional Friday-night delivery driver. She over-tipped him, as usual, and told him to "stay warm out there" as she took the big, hot boxes into her arms and hustled back to the kitchen. Even before she could place them on the counter, the bell rang again, and she rushed back to find Camilla and Mila, the first of her sisters to arrive. Within the next five minutes, Jennifer and Olivia arrived, too.

It had been a while since the girls had been all together. As they dug into the pizza, Jennifer tried to remember the last time.

"It must have been around when we discovered that weird chest in the basement of the mansion," she said, as strings of cheese oozed up from the pie and smeared across her plate.

"That's right! The chest with absolutely nothing of value in it," Mila said with a laugh. "That pole nearly took me out."

"Nothing of monetary value, sure," Olivia said. "But those diaries and books and old photographs are really something to see."

"You're an old softie, Olivia," Amelia told her. "This is the perfect kind of treasure for you. You're just swimming in your own nostalgia."

"True," Olivia said with a laugh. "Although I think Anthony's helped with that a lot. Living in the here and now and all that jazz."

"You guys are adorable together," Amelia offered.

"Chelsea won't stop teasing me about him," Olivia said. "She says I'm acting even more like a teenager than she is. It's true that I do change my outfit at least three times before I go over to the house even though all I do once I get there is spackle and sweat and eat pasta and drink wine."

"I would give anything for that," Mila offered. "I went on another dud date the other day."

"No way!" Jennifer cried. "When were you going to tell us? You know, we have that group chat for a reason."

"I know. I know. I just felt embarrassed to go on a date with a guy from an app," Mila said as her cheeks reddened. "I mean, is this what my life's come to?"

"It's modern. It's just what people do," Jennifer affirmed.

"It's not what you did, Jen," Mila said pointedly. "Derek just walked into your life, tried to ruin it, and then decided to fall in love with you instead."

"We can't all get as lucky as Jen," Amelia said with a crooked grin.

"Oh, but some of us did get lucky recently," Olivia blurted out. Almost immediately, she smacked her palm over her lips. She'd given up the goose.

The conversation died immediately. Jennifer, Mila, Amelia, and Camilla all gaped at Olivia, who remained there with her hand over her mouth. Her eyes flashed to Amelia and then the girls. "Crap." That was all she said.

Finally, Camilla said, "What do you mean? Who's gotten lucky recently?"

It wasn't like them to keep secrets from one another. Admittedly, Amelia hadn't meant to keep her one-night stand from them — it had just gotten lost in the chaos of her mind the previous few weeks. In some respects, it felt like a long time ago.

"Someone's got a secret!" Jennifer said with a bright smile. "Come on. Out with it!"

"Let's smoke it out," Mila said as she rubbed her palms together.

"Who's to say it isn't your secret?" Jennifer said. "You look mischievous like you want to pin the blame on anyone else."

"I just told you! I had a bad date," Mila said with a shrug. "No way was I going back home with that guy."

Jennifer's eyes turned from Mila to Camilla to Olivia before they landed on Amelia. Amelia felt it: embarrassment, creeping in the form of a blush, all the way from her chest to her upper cheeks.

"No." Jennifer exhaled as her eyes widened. "Amelia Taylor. Did you go on an actual date with a human male?"

Amelia rolled her eyes. "You say it like it's so outside the bounds of reason."

Jennifer leaped from the couch, very nearly casting her plate of pizza to the floor. "And you say it like it isn't something to be celebrated! Oh my, gosh, Amelia! Workaholic Amelia! You went on a date! Tell us everything! Spill the beans!"

To Amelia's surprise, she actually took a bit of pleasure in explaining the situation to her girlfriends. She talked about the minor car accident, about the handsome man who'd called her up that evening after Mandy's cheerleading accident, and then about their strange date at the Oak Bluffs bar.

"I just sat there thinking, is this really what people do? On purpose?" Amelia said as she took another cheesy slice from the grease-laden box. "I had zero idea of what to say to him. Luckily, he seemed pretty experienced in the land of women, so." She shrugged. "He came up with enough topics. And then, the gin and tonics made my tongue a bit looser."

"I guess that came in handy a little bit later," Mila teased as she waggled her eyebrows.

Amelia was pretty sure her face was full-on tomato-red. "He took me back to the Sunrise Cove, of all places."

"More memories at the Sunrise Cove!" Jennifer said. "You really have to tell Susan that you got laid there."

Amelia rolled her eyes. "I'm pretty sure they all know. Not that it matters. But I did have a little walk of shame through the foyer."

The girls laughed uproariously at that.

"Amelia Taylor on a walk of shame!" Camilla cried. "I actually thought you'd never have to go through that."

"I guess I'm getting my wild years out of my system after forty," Amelia said.

"Good for you," Jennifer said, her eyes bright.

Amelia remembered the shame she had felt the following day when she'd collapsed at Olivia's mansion and explained the inner aching of her heart. Somehow, all that felt so far away. She could acknowledge the humor in the story, now. She felt bigger than it.

"Did it make you want to try to date more?" Camilla asked. "Asking out of pure research. I have no idea if I'll ever feel ready to date, now that I'm — ugh — single."

Amelia shook her head. "To be honest, going out with Nathan Gregory gave me a picture of the male species that I don't care to look at again. And then, almost immediately after that, I met this other horrible man, a developer guy, who wants to build up a little resort and refuses to get together the relevant permits. He talks to me like I'm just this little stone he keeps stepping on."

"Which developer guy?" Jennifer asked.

"His name is Oliver Krispin," Amelia said.

Jennifer chewed her lower lip contemplatively. "I actually think Derek has mentioned him."

"Remember what he thought of him?" Amelia asked.

"I don't think he has that much respect for him, to be honest," Jennifer said. "But I can tell you more later."

"The guy actually thought I wouldn't notice that he hadn't cleared breaking ground with the environmental groups," Amelia said as her eyes narrowed. "Just proof that these self-assured, rich guys come onto this island and want to kick us Islanders around. I won't stand for it."

"Everyone except Derek," Jennifer corrected with a funny smile.

"Again, who knows what kind of evil he might have concocted, if only he hadn't fallen head over heels with our Jennifer," Olivia said.

Once they'd stuffed themselves with pizza, Amelia paraded back into the kitchen and prepped bowls of ice cream for her girls. There, in the silence of herself, she listened as they continued to laugh and gossip and tease one another. In some ways, they sounded just the same as they had some twenty years ago. Only Michelle's voice was missing. Oh, how they always missed her, no matter how much time went by.

Amelia couldn't help but feel her heart swell with pride. Over the previous ten years, the only news she'd been able to bring her sisters had everything to do with Mandy, Jake, Daniel and her parents. She'd never had anything personal and private to share — nothing good and nothing bad.

Now, with news of Nathan Gregory, she felt as though she had joined the ranks of the living. One night stand or not, she was still a woman, a wanted, beautiful, confident woman. She wanted to channel that energy for the rest of her life.

CHAPTER TEN

MANDY AGREED to meet Amelia at the same lunch spot at the same time the following afternoon. Amelia dressed in another stellar outfit. A jean dress with an intricate lace collar, knee-high boots, and eyeliner and mascara that made her eyes pop splendidly. When she sat at the same lunch table, she crossed and uncrossed her legs and tapped her finger on the table as the minutes passed by. What was it about this spring that made her want to dress her best?

Mandy was late. At first, it was only five minutes and then, the time drifted toward ten after. Amelia checked her texts to make sure she had the time correct. Naturally, just as ever, she did. They'd confirmed twice — once last night and once this morning.

AMELIA: Hey honey! Are you okay?

AMELIA: I got us a table. Want me to order for you?

The texts went through, but nobody read them on the other side. Amelia's heart thudded in her chest. When her clock read seventeen after, she felt it was time to take action. None of this was like Mandy.

She lifted a hand and gestured toward the waiter. "I'm terribly sorry. Something has come up, and I need to head out. Can I please still tip you?"

The waiter said it wasn't a problem, even as Amelia flipped a five-dollar bill onto the table and rushed out into the light breeze of the early afternoon. She rushed toward her car, her eyes still on her phone—still, no word from Mandy.

The drive toward Daniel's house took much longer than it normally did. It was Saturday, and the sky was a ridiculous, robin's egg blue, which seemed to draw out walkers and bikers and vehicles in droves. Amelia pressed a hand on her steering wheel as she waited behind a particularly thick-headed driver, who seemed not to know the difference between red and green on the stoplight.

Finally, Amelia pulled into Daniel's driveway. Normally, Daniel worked at the museum on Saturdays, and Jake was often off with friends or else at the gym for practice. Amelia snuck her key into the front doorknob as she tried to shove away a million horrible thoughts about what could have transpired that morning.

When she entered, the house was silent. Jake's basketball shoes sat, stinking slightly, in the foyer, alongside Daniel's hiking ones and Mandy's little, jeweled flats.

"Hello?" Amelia called. As she walked, she thought back to long-ago days, right after Suzy had taken off for New York, when she'd entered the house like this to find Mandy and Jake in states of panic, either screaming or crying or both.

"Hello?" she called again.

The kitchen was messy, but not overly so. Three cereal bowls sat in the sink, with the slightest bit of milk in their bottoms. Without thinking, Amelia scrubbed the bowls and placed them on the drying rack. She then took a washcloth to the countertops. As she went after a sticky area near the fridge, she remembered a long-ago afternoon with Suzy when Mandy had been maybe four or five years old. "I'm not domestic," Suzy had said. "I don't know what I was thinking, getting pregnant like that. Kind of stupid, huh?" She'd then taken a big sip of her wine and cackled.

Amelia hadn't known what to say.

At that moment, Amelia's phone buzzed with a message from Jennifer.

JENNIFER: I asked Derek about that guy. Oliver Krispin. Apparently, he has a bad reputation for coming into places and taking away their integrity.

Amelia laughed inwardly.

AMELIA: Sounds like him. Not on my watch, though. Not on the Vineyard.

JENNIFER: Thank goodness the island has you.

Amelia wandered toward Mandy's bedroom after that. Her mind swam with confusion. She had long-since known this about herself: that she was sometimes overly protective of her niece and nephew, of her best friends, and even of Martha's Vineyard itself. She had to be in control all the time; she felt she knew best in most respects. Maybe this was stupid of her. Maybe it was the only way to live.

Mandy's door was latched shut. The slightest buzz of music came out from under the door. Mandy had never been the kind of girl to lock herself away, but pregnancy did strange things to a person. Amelia knew this after watching all her dearest friends go through it. She lifted her knuckles and rapped gently. Then, after a few minutes of silence, she knocked again.

"Mandy?" she called, as tenderly as she could. "Mandy, I was worried about you. I wanted to come to make sure you're okay."

Again, silence. After a moment, Mandy turned down the music. It felt like Amelia stood on the other side of a tomb.

"Mandy, I'll leave if you want me to," she tried, although she really didn't mean it. "Just let me know that you're okay."

Finally, the door creaked open. Amelia tried her best not to change her face in alarm. The smell of rotting food and dirty laundry swarmed over her. Her eyes flashed with shock at the sight of Mandy. The cheerleading star was normally so spick and span and beautiful, but now, her hair was greasy, she wore her father's pajama pants, and there was a massive stain on her sweatshirt. She looked at Amelia with eyes that belonged to a ghost, not a teenaged girl.

"I'm sorry," Mandy said softly. Her lower lip quivered. "I'm sorry I missed lunch."

Amelia wanted to laugh at how silly that sounded. How stupid lunch was when compared to everything else! She stepped into the grey light of the bedroom and pushed the door closed behind her. Mandy collapsed back at the edge of the bed and dug a Twizzler from a bag. She ate the edge of it somberly and stared down at the floor.

"You really didn't have to come all the way over here," Mandy said.

"Of course I did." Amelia laughed and then added, "And you know everything in Edgartown is about five minutes away from everything else."

Mandy gave a sad shrug. She then lifted the bag of Twizzlers to offer Amelia one. She took one of the rubbery sugary snacks and then sat next to Mandy. Again, she inhaled a bit too much and acknowledged the stench of the room.

"Everything is such a mess," Mandy whispered.

Amelia placed her hand across Mandy's upper back and rubbed at the tense muscles near her neck. The girl was on an emotional rollercoaster, and it had only just begun. Probably, it would last the rest of her life.

"Did you talk to your dad?" Amelia asked, wondering if this was the reason for the depressive episode.

Mandy shook her head. "No. And I haven't even told Colin about the baby, either."

"Colin?"

"The father," Mandy turned to look at her aunt. "He's a senior and headed to Yale. I'm pretty sure he won't want to stick around for some baby."

Amelia's heart darkened. How unfair it was that this boy was allowed this bright future while Mandy tried to rot herself away in this bedroom.

"But you have to tell him sometime," Amelia advised.

"I guess."

The silence stretched between them. For the first time since Suzy had left, Amelia felt at a complete loss for words.

"I just wanted to hear it from her," Mandy said suddenly.

Amelia's ears perked up. "What do you mean?"

Mandy dragged a finger beneath her eye to mop up a tear. "I hadn't talked to her since my sixteenth birthday."

Oh. Amelia knew immediately who Mandy referred to.

Her own mother. Suzy.

"She was in the middle of something when I first called her last night, so I called her back this morning. Early. Between her jog and her yoga session," Mandy explained. Her words were sour. "I could hear the sound of the city in the background. It sounded so alive, full of noise. And her voice was bright and chipper and somehow rich if that's even a thing a voice can be? Like you can just hear the fact that they live in one of those high-rise apartment buildings near Central Park."

Mandy sniffled as Amelia rubbed her upper shoulders harder.

"She asked me what I needed. As though I wasn't allowed to just call my own mother when I felt like it," Mandy said. "I mean, we're kind of strangers, and I know that. But she did live in this house for like ten years with me. Ten years is a hell of a long time."

"It really is."

"Anyway. I kind of skirted around the point for a while. I asked her about her stupid dogs. I asked her about Manhattan. She was happy to tell me all about the party she and that idiot husband of hers threw last weekend and about how much money they spent on champagne alone. She rattled on about that for a long time until she finally asked me, *'Hey, so, how's senior year?'* Honestly, I was surprised she even remembered I'm about to graduate high school. I kind of told her that I was almost done with cheerleading, and she remarked that I was always so flexible, as though she was actually impressed with that. I do remember saying, *'Mom! Watch me!'* and doing cartwheels in the backyard. Probably, she didn't watch me. Probably, she just drank herself silly and then got mad at Dad and found reasons to fight with him. Guaranteed, that's how it went. Anyway, listen to me. I'm totally losing steam."

Amelia's throat constricted with sorrow. Mandy hadn't spoken of her mother over the years, not a great deal, and it pained Amelia to know that Mandy carried around these memories, as kind of "proof" to herself that maybe, just maybe, she wasn't enough for Suzy. That she'd never been enough.

"Finally, I asked her, though. I figured, what the heck? I've lost everything else, so I might as well just ask her. 'Why did you leave us? How could you just up and leave your children?'

"She didn't answer for a few seconds. I could tell the questions threw her off. But she finally said that she knew right after me and Jake were born that she wasn't fully cut out to be a mother. That God had other plans for her. Can you believe she actually said that about God?"

Mandy turned her eyes toward Amelia's. They were brimmed with tears that she couldn't control any longer. Her heart ached for her niece and Amelia couldn't understand how a mother could do that. Ever.

Amelia furrowed her brow. "You can't think that what your mother did was the right thing to do. It was completely selfish. It was not God's plan. It wasn't anyone's plan but her own. Do you understand that?"

Mandy's shoulders quaked and she nodded. "I'm just so worried, Aunt Amelia. What if I take one look at this baby and realize what my mother knew about herself? What if I turn out just like her? What if I blame my baby for everything that goes wrong in my life and then take off?"

Amelia wrapped her arms around Mandy as she shook against her. Her heart surged with anger. In fact, she'd never hated Suzy more than she hated her at this moment. She could almost handle the fact that Suzy had left, abandoning her children, but she couldn't take the idea that she had put doubt in Mandy's own mind about her ability to be a mother.

When Amelia leaned back, she made full eye contact with her niece and whispered, "I knew your mother well, Mandy. I knew her as an adult in ways that you couldn't have known her. And I've watched you grow up from day one. The only thing I know for sure is this. You are about a hundred times stronger than your mother ever was. She's a weak person. She could be lovely, even wonderful, at times. But she didn't have the strength to stick around. I know for a fact that you will. You're one of the strongest people I've ever known."

Over the next few hours, Amelia and Mandy spoke only intermittently as they cleaned her bedroom, did a load of laundry, and made a healthy lunch. So much had been said and so much had been revealed that menial conversation seemed lackluster.

Once, as Mandy stabbed a tomato with her fork, she said, "I'm sorry I didn't show enough interest in your date last week. I really am so happy you went out."

Amelia gave her a sad smile. "It's understandable that you didn't have the mental energy to think about it. And even though it was the tiniest bit traumatic, I have to say that I'm grateful I went. I think I proved something to myself."

Mandy nodded somberly. "I guess that's all we can do. We need to push ourselves to be more than we were the day before."

"Always so much wiser than your years," Amelia said, smiling at her.

"And yet, too dumb to use protection," Mandy replied with a laugh.

Mandy admitted she had to take a nap around four. Amelia watched as the girl tumbled between the clean sheets and wrapped herself up tight in her comforter. As Amelia eased back toward the front door, she watched as Jake and a few of his friends rushed down the road, tossing a football between them. You could feel it in their every movement that they were excited for summer to approach, and they would take pleasure in every moment.

Yet Mandy, poor Mandy, had to face adulthood in a very different way.

This was the nature of women, Amelia thought. They had to carry the burden of the world.

CHAPTER ELEVEN

AMELIA HEADED into the Frosted Delights Bakery the following late-morning, right in the middle of a full-fledged Sunday rush. She spotted a frazzled Jennifer across the sea of heads, her eyes focused as she tried to take down everyone's orders correctly.

"That's three caramel cappuccinos? No, one vanilla, two caramel. Got it," she said, just loud enough for Amelia to hear.

Amelia stopped at the back of the line, just outside the door, and listened to the pleasant cacophony of Edgartown and Oak Bluffs' folks' conversations. Sunday was a day for family and communion, of gratefulness, and for freshly baked donuts. Despite Amelia's continued sadness over yesterday's debacle with Mandy, she allowed herself to stir in the happiness of her surroundings.

When she arrived at the register, Jennifer managed a smile and said, "Same old Sunday order as ever?"

"You got it," Amelia said.

"Cool. I already set it aside for you," Jennifer told her. She reached for a large box of a dozen assorted donuts and placed it on the counter. "I'll put it on your tab. You tell your parents hello for me, okay?"

"I will," Amelia said.

That moment, Ariane, Jennifer's mother, appeared in her wheelchair. She'd been in the back, up to her elbows in floury dough. She grinned broadly, proof of her continued health, and said, "Tell Anita hi for me, too!"

"I will. She says she misses you," Amelia said as she gathered the box in her arms and made her way to the door.

"Tell her to come by the house," Ariane offered. "Jen won't let me work here as much as I'd like and it makes for a lot of downtime."

As Amelia walked back into the late-March sunshine, she thought back to long-ago afternoons when her best friends and their mothers had gathered together. Always a big club of Edgartown women, with bonds just as powerful as blood. Unfortunately, their mothers hadn't kept as close as Olivia, Mila, Jennifer, Camilla, and Amelia had, although their love was an ever-constant thing.

Amelia arrived at her parents' place a few minutes later. Her father yanked the box of donuts from her arms jokingly as her mother dotted a kiss on Amelia's cheek and said, "Oh, darling, you're looking entirely too thin. Promise me you'll have a protein shake before you leave. You're working yourself to death, for God sakes."

Daniel, Mandy, and Jake had gathered in the back breakfast nook, around glasses of orange juice and cups of coffee.

"You sure you don't want a cup of coffee, Mandy?" Anita asked brightly. "You were so fond of it earlier this year. Remember what she said, Danny? Milk and sugar were for suckers."

Daniel laughed appreciatively as Mandy and Amelia made eye contact. Obviously, she wasn't drinking coffee for a reason; soon, the reason would explode to the surface. Everyone in that room would have to reckon with it in a different way.

"No thanks, Grandma," Mandy declined with a small smile. "I'll just stick with orange juice."

"Good for you, honey. Coffee is just another adult addiction anyway," Daniel said as he stepped toward Amelia and gave her a side-hug. "Mandy said you stopped by yesterday?"

"I did. Not for very long, though," Amelia said as she tucked a strand of hair around her ear. "We had some fun, made some lunch and had some girl talk. Nothing major."

"You should have stuck around. We've been waiting for you to watch that new Denzel Washington movie," Daniel said. "You told us if we watched it without you, you'd never forgive us."

Amelia had almost no memory of that. "Shoot. Next weekend?" she offered, although even as she said it, she felt herself forgetting all about it again.

She sat next to Mandy and side-eyed her. She had cleaned herself up well, completely eliminated the greasy, hanging strands of hair and the sallow expression on her face. Now, she picked at her donut slowly, as though it was about to jump up off the table to bite her back. Mandy had mentioned something the previous day about her fears around a "changing body," to which Amelia had said, "It's nothing compared to the beautiful things you'll experience in motherhood. It won't matter at all."

She'd said it as though she understood it and of course, she didn't. They both knew that. At least it had sounded right in the moment.

Around noon, Jake announced he had to step out to meet a friend. His grandfather asked if the "friend" was a "girl," and Jake rolled his eyes and said, "So nosy, Grandpa," in a way that told everyone that, yes, he was off to meet a girl. This made Anita turn her eyes toward Mandy and ask, "I don't suppose there's anyone special in your life, Mandy? Maybe it's not so smart, what with graduation approaching so fast. I'm sure you'll run off somewhere and meet a guy off the island. Imagine that! Our Mandy. Off on the adventure of a lifetime. College."

Mandy's shoulders slumped, even as her voice remained bright. "Yeah. Not a good time for any of that romance stuff."

"Oh, but you'll have to find someone for prom," Anita affirmed. "It's your senior prom, after all. It will be one of the most important memories of your young life!"

After a pause, Mandy stood and nearly toppled over the table. Her fingers shook. "I'm sorry. I just...I remembered I also have to meet a friend."

Amelia stepped to the side while Daniel, Jake, and the grandparents ogled Mandy curiously. Everyone sensed she was upset, but everyone brushed it aside. They just called it "teenage angst."

Amelia walked Mandy to the door and watched as she tugged her spring jacket over her shoulder. "Do you want me to come with you?" she asked.

Mandy just shrugged, which Amelia took as proof she was needed. She hustled back to the breakfast nook to announce her departure, as well. Her mother followed her to the closet while

Mandy waited for her outside and the men continued to eat donuts — always hungry and never upset. Wasn't that the way?

"That girl is lucky to have you," her mother said as she dotted a finger against Amelia's nose. "I always tell your father. It's good you never had your own. These kids need you."

Amelia half-resented when her mother said things like this, although she knew she meant well. She tried on a false smile, then hugged her mother and said, "I'll see you later this week. I'm sure there's a basketball game on the schedule. Or baseball? That's coming up quick."

"Can't keep track of the passing days," her mother said as Amelia hustled toward the front door. "Be safe out there. I heard about your little car accident. I hate to think of you rushing through town from one meeting to another."

Amelia arched her brow as she pulled the front door open. "You heard about it? How did you hear?"

Her mother shrugged. "You know how gossip flies on this island. Didn't take me long to learn."

With that, her mother's eyes sparkled ominously as though she knew a whole lot more than just the car accident. As though she knew about Amelia's little one-night-stand.

But she was much too conservative to let on.

———

AMELIA WALKED Mandy along the water for a number of minutes. Both pushed their hands in their pockets and focused their eyes on the sweeping waves. When they reached the area near the docks, where Mandy had confessed her pregnancy the week before,

Mandy pressed her hand against her stomach and said, "I really need to go home, I think. I feel nauseous. That donut didn't do me any favors."

Amelia walked Mandy the rest of the way back to Daniel's place. She waited in the living room while Mandy went into the bathroom for a long time. When she returned, her face was pale. "I just want to take a nap. You shouldn't stay."

"I can stay," Amelia informed her solemnly.

"Don't be stupid. Go outside. It's beautiful out there," Mandy insisted. "If I didn't feel on the verge of sleeping for the next forty years, I would be out there, too."

Amelia waited for a good thirty minutes, flipping through various magazines before she headed out into the sweet, spring-time breeze. She texted Mandy as she walked, telling her to call her if she needed anything — anything at all. Mandy didn't respond. Probably, she was deep in dreamland. Amelia was grateful for that, although she felt at a complete loss. What could she do for this poor girl? What could she possibly say?

Amelia wandered back toward the docks. She felt strange, contemplative, and she gripped the wooden railing and gazed out toward the horizon line, where she spotted the Edgartown Harbor Lighthouse. It had been built in 1875 but was now just used as a museum and for private parties. To Amelia, it represented so much of the island's wonderful and vibrant history — something she was sometimes obsessive about. Even her best friends joked about Amelia and her "love of history." Back in high school, she had been content to spend hours at the library. Usually, Olivia had been up for a few hours of that, as well, although Olivia's obsession had been fiction, while Amelia had loved the stories of the known residents of the island. That love had led to everything else — to Amelia's career at city hall and the immense love she had for the people around her.

Something caught her eye off to the left. At first, she thought it was maybe a bird or perhaps a fish at the surface of the water. But when she turned her head, she found a waving hand, attached to a sturdy-looking man, who gripped the mast of his sailboat. He beamed at her like he knew her, although that seemed impossible. Amelia hardly congregated with anyone outside of her circle of dear friends and family.

"Ms. Taylor!" the man called out.

Amelia's heart hammered as her limbs stiffened. The sailboat drew closer toward the docks, which put the man's face in better view. That moment, an arrogant yet wonderfully attractive smile, snaked from ear to car, and the breeze swept his hair back behind his ears. As his green eyes connected with hers, his name sprung to her mind.

Of course. Oliver Krispin. That horrible man.

Of course, he had a sailboat.

Amelia stepped back from the docks. She felt in "fight or flight" mode and turned on her heel, ready to head back toward Daniel's place. But before she could, Olivier waved his arm again and said, "Hold on just a second. Let me tie up."

Amelia balked. There was an urgency in his voice, something that intrigued her. Every bit of her felt fiery with anger toward him, but she kept herself there as he tied up the ropes and then sauntered down the dock, toward where she stood on the boardwalk. When he neared her, his forehead gleamed with springtime sun, and she noted just how white and crisp his sailing uniform was. He reeked of money, but there was something so animalistic, so physical about him, especially out here, outside the walls of Amelia's office. Amelia had to force herself to breathe.

"Amelia," Oliver said as he beamed at her. "Thank you for waiting."

Amelia crossed her arms over her chest. "I'm surprised you're here. I figured you would spend the rest of the week scrambling for relevant permits," she said pointedly.

Oliver's smile widened. "You don't miss a beat, do you?"

"I don't know what you mean."

Oliver cackled. "You know, of all the islands I've built on and all the people I've come up against, you're about the most difficult. I thought this would be like the others. Sign a few documents, and then, boom! A new resort. Everyone's happy. But you put up the barriers right away. You don't like me. You don't care about my money." He clucked his tongue and then added, "I have to say. I kind of like that about you."

Amelia flared her nostrils. "I don't care whether you like me or not."

"I'm sure you don't," Oliver replied quickly. "But you'll be happy to hear that I've decided to give up. You won't let me push the rules, and I just don't see any way to move forward on the property. You get the news straight from me, which I'm sure gives you a whole lot of pleasure."

Amelia certainly hadn't expected this. She arched an eyebrow and tried to drum up some kind of response. Everything felt lackluster.

"Well, anyway," Oliver said. He palmed the back of his neck and glanced back toward his sailboat. "I guess I'll head to

Nantucket. I haven't broken ground there yet, and I heard they're a bit more flexible."

"I wish you well on your mission to destroy as much of our natural world as you can," Amelia shot suddenly, now totally unable to hold back her tongue. "I only hope there's someone like me on Nantucket. Someone to get in your way."

Olivier chuckled. "I can tell you; there's nobody like you. Not anywhere."

Although Amelia appreciated the compliment, she still detested its source. She turned her eyes back toward the horizon line, even as she felt Oliver's gaze upon her face.

After a long, strange, pregnant pause, Oliver spoke.

"Why don't you head out with me?"

Amelia yanked her head back around in pure shock. "What do you mean? To Nantucket?"

Oliver shook his head. "No. I mean, in a more immediate sense. Why don't you come out on the boat? It's chilly, but the sun is shining and it's beautiful out there. I have some extra blankets on board, and you don't even have to talk to me if you don't want to."

"I really can't," Amelia blurted. The thought, in and of itself, was ridiculous.

But Oliver, being the ever keen businessman, pushed her.

"Come on. It's the least I can do after all the trauma I put you through."

"You give yourself too much credit," Amelia returned. "You didn't put me through any trauma. I was just doing my job."

"And I was just doing mine," he returned. "Let's have one sail together—just one. And then, we can go back to our everyday lives and everyday jobs. It would mean the world to me to be able to show you how much I respect you—really."

Amelia had no idea why this man wanted this so badly. She hardly trusted him. But a final glance out toward the Nantucket Sound tugged her heartstrings. She hadn't been out in a boat in ages. And there was something appealing about being out there, so far from her everyday problems — away from Mandy, away from Amelia's perceived life failures, and away from her family, who was so "sure" that her singleness was a Godsend.

"All right," she said finally, with a funny shrug. "But if you make even a single pass at me—"

At this, Oliver burst into raucous laughter. "I respect you way too much to flirt with you. You have my word on that."

"How charming," Amelia returned.

CHAPTER TWELVE

AMELIA STEPPED LIGHTLY onto the sailboat, perched in a little white chair, which was attached to the boat itself, and watched curiously as Oliver Krispin ducked about and prepared the boat to disembark. His face was focused, terribly handsome, and his motions were urgent. With a brash yank of the rope, he fleshed out the sails and brought the boat out from the dock. There was a great feeling of being lifted, and soon, the boat glided atop the waves as sunlight glittered across Amelia's cheeks. For a moment, she was able to pretend that everything was right as rain and that she was just another of these rich, sailing elites, with the entire afternoon to devote to the waters and the sands and the sky.

They sailed east and then cut around the lighthouse to head west again. They passed the Fuller Street Beach, then swept past Eel Pond, before heading out past the Joseph Sylvia State Beach, which was a thin stretch of white sand, and one of Amelia's favorite walks, which she often did alone when she wanted to organize her thoughts.

She remembered a particularly strange walk along that stretch of beach approximately five years before, when she'd fully acknowledged her age, that of thirty-five, along with the fact that she hadn't bothered to meet anyone or have a family. Out on that strip of sand, she'd come to terms with the idea that perhaps, motherhood was not part of her future. You had to be brave to be a wife and a mother. You had to take chances.

But she'd told herself, on that day, that she was, in fact, quite brave not to do it, also. There was courage in remaining alone. At least, she had to believe that.

When they neared Oak Bluffs, they spotted one of the ferries, headed out of Woods Hole. Without thinking, Amelia lifted a hand to wave to the ferry passengers. Oliver laughed, and she dropped her hand to her thigh with embarrassment.

"No! No. Don't stop waving on my account," Oliver told her. He sounded genuinely sad that he had upset her. "I'm just not from the kind of place that waves to passers-by like they do here on the island. It always surprises me to see that kind of thing."

"Surprises you to see people being nice to each other?" Amelia asked, arching a brow.

He nodded as his green eyes flashed. His handsomeness was horrible, although just now, he didn't use it as a weapon. It was just how he looked.

"I guess so." He paused and then asked, "I guess you haven't spent much time off the island, have you?"

"Hardly more than a few days at a time," Amelia confessed.

Oliver formed his lips into a round O and whistled. "That's insane to me. I might have gone crazy, all cooped up here."

Amelia shrugged. "I never knew anything else."

"You're like a caged bird. You don't know what's out the window," Oliver said.

"What's out there?" Amelia asked. "Anything I should know about?"

Oliver arched an eyebrow. He then turned his nose out toward the rolling waves, the glorious bright blue horizon line. He closed his eyes, exhaled slowly, and said, "No. You're right. There's nothing out there like Martha's Vineyard. Stay in your cage, little bird."

Amelia laughed and was surprised to hear the happiness behind it. Sure, this man was terribly arrogant and far too handsome for his own good, but at least he was semi-clever. That was a rare thing.

As they swept westward toward Makonikey, Oliver poured them glasses of champagne. Amelia accepted the glass but didn't take a sip. She watched as the bubbles crept up the side of the glass, as Oliver spoke longingly about Martha's Vineyard and all the years he'd wanted to be a part of it. For some reason, Amelia's thoughts spun toward Michelle, that long-ago day when they'd lost her off the back of the boat in the middle of the night. It was strange how she carried that tragedy around with her. In some ways, she remembered almost everything about Michelle. She remembered the funny laugh she'd had, one completely different from Jennifer's, and she remembered her courage, which seemed to stretch over every possible thing. But in other ways, Amelia had to reckon with the fact that she lost memories of Michelle almost every day.

Michelle's memory was probably just an echo of an actual memory, now — stories Amelia and her best friends had told one another too many times so that they'd taken on lives of their own.

Again, Oliver whistled. "Yoo-hoo!"

Amelia blinked up to find him directly over her. "You okay?" he asked.

Amelia realized she'd spaced out. She pressed her palm across her forehead and passed her glass of champagne over to Oliver. "Sorry. It's been a weird few weeks. I don't know if I'm totally here." She was surprised at her honesty with him; in what world did he deserve it?

Oliver sipped her glass of champagne, having completed his own, and said, "Don't worry. You can use this time however you want."

The words were so kind, so outside of the personality she'd attributed to Oliver Krispin, that Amelia furrowed her brow in shock. Oliver said nothing more. He instead stepped over toward another sail to adjust it, leaving Amelia with her gorgeous view of the island as they churned past. It looked remarkable, just a glowing rock beneath the sun.

The sail felt meditative. Amelia gave in to the splendor of the island's beauty. Her eyes sparkled at the sight of Aquinnah Cliffs, which Oliver admitted aloud he'd never seen. "Look at those," he breathed. "I normally don't sail in this direction."

"They're really something, aren't they?" Amelia beamed. "When me and my friends used to hike out here, we would stand on that rock and scream out across the waters."

Oliver's eyes glittered as he eyed the top of the rocks. "What did you scream?"

Amelia was surprised he cared. She paused for a moment, then said, "I think we screamed what we wished for. We believed that something lived in the water. Something or someone who could fulfill our wishes."

"Do you remember what you wished for?"

Amelia bit hard on her lower lip. She could actually hear all their screams now, as though the six of them still stood on top of that cliff and yelled out their hopes.

Jennifer had cried out for Joel's babies and she had been given a son.

Michelle had cried out for absolute freedom. Amelia supposed, in a sense, that's what she'd been given.

Olivia had cried out to be a famous writer one day.

Mila had jokingly asked to be beautiful for the rest of her life. Even now, she was the most perfect-looking woman Amelia knew, and she owned an esthetician salon. In a sense, she hadn't needed the ocean or its wildness to cling to her beauty, but who was to say she hadn't needed a bit of help?

But what had Amelia screamed for?

"I guess you don't?" Oliver asked as the silence stretched between them.

Amelia clucked her tongue. "I can remember what all of my friends said. But for me? I don't even know. What did I want back then?" She buzzed her lips and then found a way to laugh about it. "I don't know. But do you remember what you wanted back then? Age sixteen, seventeen, or eighteen?"

Oliver considered her words carefully. He then smacked his hand against the mast of the sailboat and said, "I went on vacation as a kid, and I saw this guy out on a sailboat. I told myself I would have one someday. One way or another."

"Even if you had to lie and steal and cheat your way there?" Amelia asked, half-teasing.

Oliver laughed. "I know it might shock you to hear this, but I didn't lie or steal or cheat to get this sailboat."

"It does shock me." She grabbed the sails pole as she giggled just a little.

"Well, I can tell you, it was a whole lot of hard work. And college and grad school. And days wondering if I would ever make my money back after a bad investment."

"Sounds like a lot of stomach aches," Amelia offered.

"That's one way to put it."

Amelia tilted her head and allowed herself to see something else in his face: a kind of sorrow. She wondered where it had come from. Was he really alone in the world? Where did he call "home" these days? Or was home just wherever he woke up the following day, ready to rip through the ground to build a new luxury resort?

When they neared the Edgartown Great Pond, neither of them spoke. This was the area where Oliver had wanted to build his little resort — the beautiful space between the ocean and the pond itself, just west of Crackatuxet Cove. Oliver's face was wistful as they passed by.

Finally, Oliver said something a bit too quiet so that Amelia strained to hear.

"What was that?"

Oliver tried again, but again, the wind whipped between them, and Amelia couldn't make out his words. After the third time,

Amelia burst into laughter, and Oliver joined her. As if on cue, the wind stopped then, and they could hear one another.

"I would say it again," Oliver said as he gasped for air, "But I'm pretty sick of it, myself."

Amelia chuckled. "Hey. Do you want to know a fun fact about Martha's Vineyard?"

"Uh oh. Is this where your really nerdy qualities come out?"

"Yes."

"Okay. I'll allow it. Just this once," he said.

Amelia arched her brow. She couldn't help but sense that he now flirted with her, despite his promise that he wouldn't. But was she enjoying it? Did she possibly like it too much to call him out?

"Okay. Here it is. A big Martha's Vineyard fact," Amelia said as she delivered a goofy smile. "The island was once home of one of the earliest known deaf communities in the United States. This was all the way back in the late 1600s. Way before the US became a country. Back then, they developed a Martha's Vineyard-only sign language, which was used before American Sign Language was even invented. Isn't that crazy?"

"What did you say?" Oliver said, teasing her.

"Ha," Amelia shot back, rolling her eyes. "But come on. Isn't that fascinating?"

Oliver's eyes caught hers for a long time. She couldn't look away. She was totally captivated with him, although she would never, not in a million years, tell him that. She supposed she was drunk — not on alcohol, as she hadn't had a single sip but on the water, the sun, the sky and the conversation. It was so, totally outside the bounds of what she normally did.

And it filled her with a sense of longing for something much more.

Oliver drove the sailboat back up Katama Bay, back up toward the docks. When Amelia stepped off the boat, her knees clacked together uncontrollably, and Oliver hopped up onto the dock to ensure she didn't fall back. His hand cupped her elbow to steady her, and the heaviness of his grip against her made her spine shiver.

After another long silence, Amelia cleared her throat and said, "That was really something. Thank you for taking me out."

"Of course," Oliver said. "It was my pleasure. I told you. You're one of the most fascinating and bull-headed creatures I've ever met in my life."

A blush crept up through Amelia's chest, her neck, and up through her cheeks. She simply couldn't trust her body not to give her away.

"Why don't you come to dinner with me?" Oliver said then as he yanked the rope into an intricate knot.

"You think that little knot maneuver is enough to impress a girl like me?" Amelia said.

Oliver gave her a big-eyed look. "You think I'd only tie up my boat to impress a woman?"

Amelia shrugged as yet another blush encroached on her face. Maybe he hadn't actually asked her out? Maybe she'd misunderstood?

But then, that now-familiar arrogant smile crept up toward his ear. "Come on. Really. Dinner on me."

Amelia took a delicate step back. She felt pulled in the opposite direction. After all, that one-night stand with Nathan Gregory had been enough and she wasn't prepared to be seated across from yet another arrogant guy, no matter how many drinks he agreed to purchase for her. She'd had enough fun.

"Thanks for the ride, but I have to head back home," Amelia said. "My schedule is packed tomorrow with other millionaires who want to destroy the island."

"Ah. Then you'd better rest up to deal with them," Oliver said. He reached for the zipper on his jacket and yanked it to his chin. "I know it won't take those others long to recognize that you're a force to be reckoned with. Unless, of course, they're stupid."

Amelia laughed aloud as she turned back toward the boardwalk. "Good night, Oliver Krispin. Get back to wherever you came from safe, won't you? And don't let the metaphorical door hit you on your way out."

CHAPTER THIRTEEN

DAYS CREPT FORWARD, just as they always had before. The only real darkness that hung over Amelia's head these days was the knowledge that soon, she and Mandy would have to make real, life-altering decisions regarding her pregnancy. Daniel would have to be told; doctor's appointments would have to be made; college would have to be pushed back. It was a lot to think about, but, as Amelia tried to translate as much as she could to Mandy, they could handle it, just as they'd handled everything else before.

Amelia tried her best not to think about the fact that Mandy had called her mother. It was strange to think of this woman, who'd given birth to both Jake and Mandy, just off gallivanting through Manhattan, eager to tell her eldest that she "just wasn't cut out" to be a mother. Amelia strained herself not to call the woman up herself and give her a piece of her mind.

On Thursday of the following week, Amelia received several

messages from Mandy. Amelia bent over her desk, between one meeting and the next, and read Mandy's words.

MANDY: I think Colin suspects something's up.

MANDY: Since I won't talk to him.

MANDY: But also, because I keep leaving the classroom to throw up. That might have something to do with it, too.

Amelia's head felt heavy with sorrow. As she lifted her phone to answer with words of compassion, she heard a rap at her office door. Ordinarily, her secretary bustled in and out at-will. This time, however, the hand behind this knock seemed masculine and powerful. Amelia lifted her chin and said, "Come in?"

At that moment, her boss, Zane, appeared in the doorway. He looked strangely bloated, as though he'd had a hard night out at the bar and hadn't yet recovered, and it was clear, from his midriff, that he needed to purchase a belt with an extra bit of leather. He glowered at Amelia as though she was an obstinate student and he was the principal. Naturally, this seemed off since Amelia did about ten times the amount of work he did.

"Zane. Hello," Amelia said, forcing a fake smile. "What can I do for you?"

"Amelia, could I have a word?"

His voice was cold and somber. Amelia set her phone on the desk, crossed her arms over her chest, and said, "Absolutely. What's up?"

"Perhaps in my office?"

"I'm on my way somewhere, Zane," Amelia said. "My schedule is about as jam-packed as always. Do you mind just telling me right here?"

Zane glanced back toward Amelia's secretary. He looked nervous, and the color drained from his cheeks as he stepped into her office and pushed the door closed. Amelia's head stirred with curiosity. It wasn't like Zane to be so confrontational.

"Sit down, please, Amelia," he said, gesturing toward her chair.

"I can stand, thank you. Like I said, I'm on my way somewhere."

"I would really prefer it if you sat."

Amelia half-rolled her eyes. In the back of her mind, she again assessed the number of humdrum tasks she'd had to do for him over the years, as he'd struggled with scheduling, staying organized, and getting to places on time. He was her cross to bear, in human form.

"Okay," Amelia said in annoyance. She tipped herself into her chair to sit just at the edge. She then folded her fingers on the desk and blinked at him. In a steady voice, she said, "What can I do for you, Zane?"

Zane reached into his back pocket, gripped a handkerchief, and dabbed his nose. "Amelia, something pretty dreadful has come to my attention."

"Oh? You just saw that pothole on Main Street? I have a crew headed there later today," Amelia said with a cheeky smile.

This seemed to fluster him even more. He glanced toward the ground and then added. "Thank you for that. Yes, I've heard a few complaints about the pothole."

"Don't mention it, boss." Amelia nodded with a smile.

He then cleared his throat. "I took it upon myself this morning to investigate where we stood with the Oliver Krispin project."

Amelia's heart jumped slightly. "Yes."

"And I see that it hasn't moved forward. At all, in fact."

"No. It hasn't."

"So I went ahead and called him," Zane continued. "And he mentioned that he was unable to get together the appropriate paperwork. I have to say that I was floored when he said that. Because isn't it your job, Amelia, to ensure that men like him find ways through some of these bigger obstacles?"

Amelia arched her brow. "It was my understanding that it was my job to keep the island of Martha's Vineyard's interests at heart above everything else. Above, most definitely, the affairs and interests of some overly rich man from the city."

With every word that Amelia spoke, Zane seemed to grow in his anger. He lifted his shoulders toward his ears and then said, "Amelia. We discussed this at length. His resort was staged to bring in a huge amount of money to this island. It wasn't something to scoff at."

"And I didn't scoff at it," Amelia retorted. "He didn't bring in the relevant paperwork. Permits are required to build in certain areas, as you know."

"Yes, but Amelia. We have the power to push past some of those rules."

"And why on earth would we do that?"

Zane puffed out his cheeks. Amelia thought that maybe if she didn't tell him to breathe, he might collapse to the ground.

"Amelia. You know this island better than anyone."

"I would say so, yes."

"And then, you know that these resorts and this industry, this gives the people of Martha's Vineyard a number of jobs. We need these places to keep going."

"I know that very well. But he planned to build in a protected area. The wildlife of Martha's Vineyard is my responsibility, as well. And, Zane, if I might add — it's your responsibility, too."

"You don't have to tell me what my responsibility is, Ms. Taylor." His words were dangerous, now. He looked like a dragon, on the verge of blowing fire.

"I know that," Amelia said softly, although, in actuality, she hadn't seen Zane do much of anything in years.

"In fact, I feel that you've gotten a bit too big for your britches as of late, Ms. Taylor."

Amelia wanted to laugh. Instead, she asked, "What do you mean?"

"I mean that you think you have much more responsibility than you do," Zane continued. "The fact that you never consulted me about this permit issue is certainly worrying."

Amelia had about a million responses to that — like, for example, the fact that Zane was hardly ever in his office or available for such "consultation."

"Excuse me?" she finally mustered.

"You heard me," Zane replied. "You made the island of Martha's Vineyard lose out on the potential of hundreds of thousands of dollars in revenue. And you did it without a second thought."

"Hang on. You know that I do everything with a second thought. Or even a triple thought."

"No. You've gone too far, Amelia. This time, I can't just sit back and let you pretend you run the show," Zane sputtered. "In fact, I think I will take it upon myself to call Oliver Krispin back to the island. And I think it would be best that, while Mr. Krispin and I arrange breaking ground on the new resort, you take a leave of absence. This will give both you and I time to consider your role here and what exactly it should look like in the future."

Amelia's jaw nearly dropped to the floor.

A leave of absence?

What did that even mean?

That was something that happened to other people. Amelia had gotten all the way through middle school and high school without a single detention. She'd never once gotten into trouble. Her parents had always called her "the golden child," and Daniel had never even refuted it. Since she'd gotten her job at city hall, she had hardly missed a single day of work and had hardly bothered at all with dating, which meant she'd never really found Mr. Right. Her life had been tied up at city hall.

And now, where would she take that life?

"You have to be kidding me, Zane," she said, hardly loud enough for her own ears to hear it.

"If you think I'm kidding, then you're sorely mistaken," Zane shot back. He then cut back toward the door, where he paused with his hand on the knob. "Make sure you share your schedule with one of your colleagues to make sure we don't miss any relevant meetings."

And with that, he stomped out into the hallway and left Amelia all alone.

With every moment that passed, Amelia's confusion mounted. She placed her files back in her folder and then lifted the folder to her chest. On second thought, she placed the folder in a drawer as she realized the meeting she'd been heading to would now have to be rescheduled. It was somebody else's problem.

Even the pothole on Main Street was someone else's problem.

Her heart dropped into her stomach as she reached for her coat. Zane's words echoed through her skull. Had she really overstepped her position? Had she actually gotten too egotistical to perform her job correctly?

When Amelia appeared in the foyer, her secretary peered at her curiously.

"Shouldn't you be on your way to that meeting?" she asked.

Amelia tilted her head as her eyes filled with tears. "Actually, could you please call them and reschedule? Give them Zane's number. It's — it's up to Zane, now."

Her secretary laughed at that. "Right. Is it up to Zane? Then all of Martha's Vineyard will go up in flames."

But a moment later, her secretary realized the serious tone of Amelia's voice. She stood slowly, her eyes focused on Amelia's.

"Amelia, you're not serious, are you? What is going on?"

Amelia just shook her head somberly. "You'll need to reschedule all of my meetings this week. Pass them off to others, or ask them to wait until — until I'm —"

She couldn't bear to say it. Her fate was in Zane's hands. He'd taken everything from her.

When Amelia stepped out of the building, she realized that her vehicle wasn't in the parking lot. She'd taken it to be repaired that morning, as it had been far too long since her strange accident with Nathan Gregory. When she'd placed the keys in the guy's black-stained hands, she'd told herself: *The nightmare is over. Your light will be fixed, and you can get on with your life now.*

Ah. But the nightmare had apparently only just begun.

Amelia walked toward the center of Edgartown in a kind of daze. The days had drifted toward the end of March, and there was a strange humidity to the air. She blinked up to catch the brewing dark clouds, which steamed over the bright blue stretch of sky. Rain approached, and she was nothing if not ill-prepared. She remembered her umbrella, where it still hung on the coat rack in her office. She thought to turn around and head back up to grab it, but the last face she wanted to see was her boss. God only knew what she might have done.

The first raindrops pelted her nose, her shoulders, and the top of her forehead. Her hair deflated beneath the drips, and she turned her eyes toward the sidewalk as she continued to walk on. She wasn't so far from her house, not really, and she knew the moment she arrived, she could draw a bath and weep as loud as she wanted.

After all, it wasn't like anyone was at home to hear her.

Suddenly, a horn blared directly beside her. Amelia nearly jumped from her skin as she yanked her head around to spot the driver.

Mila.

Hurriedly, Mila brought the passenger window down and called, "Amelia! What the heck are you doing out here?"

Amelia stuttered. She had absolutely no idea how to describe what had just happened.

"Are you having some kind of breakdown?" Mila demanded.

Amelia's lower lip quivered slightly as she continued to struggle not to cry.

"Don't just stand there, Amelia! Get in the dang car!"

Amelia did as she was told. She collapsed in the passenger seat as a car pulled up behind Mila and blared its horn to demand that they drive forward. Annoyed, Mila hollered out her own window, "Hold your horses!" She then reached over, gripped Amelia's hand, and said: "Whatever it is, we'll take care of it. We always do."

CHAPTER FOURTEEN

"AMELIA, you don't have to talk to me," Mila said as they eased toward Amelia's house. Raindrops splattered across the windshield, and Mila's eyes danced from the road in front of them, over toward Amelia, to keep tabs on everything at once. "I just need you to know. I'm not leaving until I get you all set up in a warm place surrounded by all your favorite snacks, okay?"

Amelia's chin quivered. She couldn't speak.

"You've spent all these years taking care of everyone else," Mila scolded. "But you probably wouldn't have called any of us about whatever this is, would you have? Good thing I found you." She then pressed a button on her dash to call her esthetician salon. "Hey. It's Mila. I need you to reschedule all of my appointments for the rest of the day. It's an emergency."

When Mila hung up, Amelia let out a deep sigh and said, "You shouldn't have rescheduled."

"What?" Mila sounded borderline angry. "Listen, Amelia. You

can't tell me what to do right now. You're the one in the catbird seat."

"I never really understood that expression," Amelia said softly as she gave Mila the slightest of smiles.

Back in her house, Mila bustled around the kitchen to prepare Amelia a cup of tea. Amelia stood with her shoulders hunched and her hair still dripping. She then found her phone and began to text Mandy back.

"What are you doing?" Mila asked. "Who are you texting?"

"Just Mandy," Amelia said.

Mila stopped dead as the kettle began to blare. "Isn't she at school? Let her teachers take care of her for once. And isn't she eighteen years old?" She buzzed her lips, annoyed.

"She needs me, Mila," Amelia said as she rubbed her eye with her index finger.

When she removed her finger, Mila furrowed her brow, annoyed, and said, "Now, look at you. You have eyeliner all over your face. And what did I tell you about rubbing your eyes?"

"Can't you just de-wrinkle me later, Mila?" Amelia asked.

Mila rolled her eyes. "I've told you, girls, over and over again. You have to take preventative measures!"

"Today isn't a day for preventative measures," Amelia said. "It's a day for tea. And brownies."

"Did someone say brownies?" Jennifer's voice rang out from the foyer as the door slammed shut behind her.

Amelia eyed Mila suspiciously. "How did you even get the news out that we were here?"

"When you went to the bathroom, I got to work."

Jennifer appeared in the kitchen with a platter of cookies,

brownies, and little pieces of cake and pie, all from the Frosted Delights. Her eyes narrowed at Amelia's appearance. Amelia knew better than most that she always looked A-okay. Obviously now, with the eyeliner streak and the wet eyes and the sagging shoulders, she hardly looked at all like herself.

"Hey honey," Jennifer said finally, as she placed the plate of goodies on the counter and wrapped Amelia up in a hug.

Amelia placed her chin on Jennifer's shoulder and shook slightly. She was reminded of being a very little girl when she'd scraped herself up after a bike accident and fallen into her mother's arms. It was a funny thing — the fact that those open arms were no longer so open when you turned forty. Sometimes, there was nothing to do but cling to yourself in the dead of night.

Just then, the front door opened again. Olivia's voice rang out, as did Camilla's. They arrived, one-after-another, to the kitchen, and together, the five of them formed a circle, with their arms wrapped around each other's shoulders.

"Look at us, all here together in the middle of the day," Olivia said brightly. Her eyes found Amelia's curiously.

"You didn't have to leave school like that," Amelia insisted.

"Oh, but I did," Olivia said. "I received the call from the sisterhood. I took the oath. We were all there."

"That's right," Jennifer affirmed. "You can't just expect that we'll ignore one of our girls when she's in trouble."

Amelia felt like a wandering, lost child. She sat on the floor of the living room while Camilla and Jennifer sat across from her. Jennifer leafed a bottle of wine from her bag and poured hearty glasses for everyone, while Mila perched on the couch behind Amelia and toyed with her hair. Olivia took a phone call from

Anthony and remained standing with her hand on her hip. "I think that dark green tile is so interesting, Anthony," she said. "It reminds me of the forties. Yes. It will look so good in that downstairs bathroom."

Amelia tried to avoid Jennifer and Camilla's eyes, even as they bore into her. She lifted her glass of wine but then returned it to the ground near her feet. She had never been particularly fond of "drinking away her problems." She didn't like losing control.

"Amelia," Jennifer said softly. She reached over and placed her hand on Amelia's knee. "You know, you can tell us anything."

"We're always going on and on about our problems," Camilla interjected.

"Seriously. We never shut up about our problems," Olivia added as she hung up the phone and slipped it into her pocket. "If something happened — with Mandy? With Daniel?"

Amelia sniffled. Again, she felt the crushing weight of what she'd potentially lost. She again lifted the glass of wine but placed it back on the ground, as she felt she just couldn't drink it.

"Zane thinks I overstepped at work," she said finally. "And he told me to take a leave of absence."

Jennifer snapped to her feet with rage. "What the hell? Are you serious?"

"That idiot never does anything!" Olivia cried. "I recently spoke to him at the grocery store, and he barely even knew about any of the projects you were hard at work on! I didn't want to mention that to you because, well, I figured you knew already what an idiot he is..."

"I know. I mean. Idiot is maybe too strong of a word, but, yeah. He really doesn't know what's happening up there. All he cares about is money. And he thinks I don't have the best interests of the island at-heart," Amelia breathed. Her hand shook as she placed it over her cheek. "I just keep thinking about all the sacrifices I made over the years for that job, you know?"

Nobody spoke as everyone stirred in the same, crazy thoughts. Amelia had never fallen in love. She'd never had her own family. Her life had been her job and then, she'd had to pick up the pieces of Daniel's failed marriage and family. Nobody wanted to say these words aloud, of course, but Amelia could see them written across each of her best friends' faces. How awful.

Why hadn't she taken just a sliver of time for herself?

Why had she allowed any of this to happen?

"I just thought I was smarter than all this," Amelia said softly.

The girls basically stumbled over themselves to attempt to fix this. Jennifer said she didn't mind going to scream at Zane if that's what it took, and Mila said she would give his wife some bad botox the next time she came to the salon.

Of course, Amelia cackled and said, "It's not her fault. Don't mess up her face, Mila. But wow. What power you have!"

"Just don't mess with my friends!" Mila muttered. "Or else."

Jennifer scrambled up a bit later to order pizza, as she'd decided that they couldn't live on brownies and cookies alone. Amelia continued to swirl her wine around and around in its glass while her sisters turned the conversation to other things. All the while, Mila rubbed at her shoulders.

After the pizza arrived, Amelia took one glance at the gooey, cheesy piece and popped to her feet to hustle to the bathroom. Once on the other side of the door, she keeled over the toilet and threw up. Outside, Jennifer was in the middle of telling a joke, and the other girls burst into laughter. None of them had noticed, and Amelia was grateful.

She'd heard of tension headaches, of throwing up due to anxiety and all of that. But she'd never actually had it happen to her. She stood and brushed her teeth to get rid of the smell, then analyzed her face in the mirror. Without the promise of a work schedule in the morning and jam-packed weeks ahead, she wasn't entirely sure who she was. She felt like a driver without GPS.

When Amelia returned to the living room, she checked her messages from Mandy, praying that Mandy needed something from her. This, she knew, was her crutch. As long as someone needed Amelia, she was valid.

MANDY: I want to tell Colin, I think. But what happens if he freaks?

AMELIA: He probably will freak.

AMELIA: You just need to ask yourself if you want this to get back to your dad before you want him to know.

AMELIA: And again, I hate lying to Daniel about all of this.

MANDY: I know. Thank you for doing it.

AMELIA: Tomorrow, I'm going to make a doctor's appointment for you, okay?

MANDY: Ugh.

AMELIA: It's time to get this process started. Make sure you're healthy.

MANDY: Ugh.

Amelia set her jaw and placed her phone back on the counter.

Her stomach continued to swirl from throwing up, but she felt much more focused, now that she had at least one thing to do tomorrow. She reached for a slice of pizza and splayed it across her plate as Camilla began to talk about a handsome stranger she'd seen on the boardwalk earlier that day while she'd been on a run.

"Listen to me," Camilla said with a smile. "I think you inspired me when you went on that date with that guy, Amelia. Now, I'm like, why am I not dating? I should be meeting people. I should be getting out there."

"Just be careful how you talk to Andrea about it," Mila said. "My Peter is dead, but my kids don't want me out dating anyone. I don't know when they'll be ready for something like that."

Amelia was grateful to fall into the easy, caring banter of her dearest friends. Occasionally, one of them asked her a question or made sure she had enough water, but mostly, they just allowed her to sit in silence. This was incredibly different than her normal mode of operation when she had to offer advice or have some kind of active participation.

Maybe she'd hit a wall.

Maybe she couldn't go forward the way she had been.

There could have been any number of reasons for all of this.

But still, she was devastated, and embarrassed, and fearful about what happened next.

What if Zane didn't offer her job back? What if she had to find another position on the island? She'd only ever wanted to do one thing in her life, and she'd been lucky enough to do just that since graduation.

But now, she was just Amelia. Single. Sad. Alone. And hungry to fix other people's problems.

CHAPTER FIFTEEN

AMELIA'S PHONE alarm blared out, just as it always did, at six in the morning. Thoughts rolled around the back of her mind as she cleared the alarm and stretched her legs out toward the edge of the bed. There was a strange heaviness to the mattress. Amelia blinked left to find beautiful blonde strands splayed out across the pillow. Camilla was tucked tightly beneath the sheets; clearly, the alarm hadn't woken her.

But why was Camilla there?

The memory of the previous day landed on her heart like an anvil. She pulled the blankets off her legs and stepped onto the chilly hardwood. Of course. She'd been forced to take a leave of absence. She had nowhere to go that morning. Nothing stopped her from diving back onto her mattress and sleeping the day away.

Her arms felt strange and heavy as she walked toward the bathroom. She felt as though she walked through an endless fog. When she reached the kitchen, she prepared a pot of coffee and watched as the black liquid dribbled into the glass container. Her stomach shifted strangely, and she burst back down the hallway to vomit, yet again, into the toilet. She tapped at her lips with a piece of toilet paper and glared at herself in the mirror. When she reached her bed again, she Googled "anxiety and vomiting," and about a million results popped up. "Try meditation," she muttered to herself. But when she closed her eyes to try to "clear her mind," she felt nothing but fear.

Where was her life going? What was any of this? How could she keep going?

One way or another, Amelia drifted off again. When she awoke, just after nine-thirty in the morning, Camilla was gone. She'd left a note on her pillow, which read: *Had to get to the hospital. Call me or the others if you need anything. Love forever. C.*

When Amelia reached the kitchen again, she poured herself a glass of water and blinked out the window. A bright red cardinal glared at her from his stance on her bird feeder, his eyes black as night and his expression stern. In just a week or two, more and more springtime birds would parade their beautiful songs from that very bird feeder. Amelia supposed she would have plenty of time to see them.

Amelia wasn't the sort of woman to just sit around and let life happen to her. There, in the kitchen, with a full stretch of time before her, she reasoned that she could finally do all the things she had neglected all these years. This meant: deep-clean the kitchen and the bathroom, rearrange her bookshelves, prepare healthy meals for the week ahead, and all that jazz. She would read every "be a better YOU" blog on the Internet, and she would, ultimately, become a better Amelia. She would be thinner, more beautiful, stronger, more organized — the kind of woman you could count on. The kind of woman who didn't just have to take a "leave of absence" due to her "personality problems."

It did her no use to blame Zane, although, of course, she wanted to so desperately. She wanted to fall into bed, eat a bag of chips, and scream her anger toward Zane to the heavens.

The clean-up, organization, alphabetization, and general 'personal betterment' lasted only a day or two. During that time, Jennifer, Olivia, Mila, and Camilla stopped by several times to keep tabs and check-in. Amelia's heart ached every time they had to return to their own lives and families. More and more, she felt the dramatic hollowness of her own life.

Three days after her leave of absence, her mother called. Without thinking, Amelia answered.

"Hey there!" her mother said. "I'm surprised I caught you. Figured you'd be in one meeting or another."

Amelia's throat constricted. In fact, she sat on her couch as a daytime talk show blared on the television in front of her. A half-eaten piece of peanut butter toast sat on a plate beside her.

"Yeah! Kind of a slow morning, I guess," Amelia said. She righted her posture on the couch as though her mother could see her.

"Well, good. You work yourself too hard," her mother said. "Listen. I wondered if you'd want to pop by for dinner tonight? Apparently, Mandy and Jake don't have anything planned, and even Daniel managed to get the night off from the museum. I would love your help making something delicious. You just have a better sense in the kitchen than I do."

"I don't think that's true," Amelia said. "But your flattery is welcome."

"When can you come?" her mother asked.

Amelia's shoulders felt heavy with loneliness. After a strange pause, she said, "Why don't I come by a little early? I can clear up my schedule later on. I could even be there by three or so?"

Her mother's voice was bright with surprise. "You don't say! Well, what made us so lucky?"

AMELIA STAGGERED through her closet to find an appropriate outfit. At first, she donned a business suit, something she would have worn to the office; this way, her parents wouldn't sense anything out of the ordinary. But as she stared at her reflection in the mirror, she felt the severity of her lie. This was a small island and everyone knew everyone else. If she kept up this lie or simply omitted the truth, it was bound to bite her in the butt.

Ultimately, she donned a sweater and a pair of jeans, added just a touch of makeup, then headed out into the bright light of a mid-afternoon in late March. It was a funny thing, not being in a rush; she felt she'd had to dart across Martha's Vineyard in her vehicle non-stop for the previous twenty years. Now, she could just walk at a gentle pace toward her parents' place. Nobody cared where she was or when she arrived.

When she arrived, her mother's face performed a number of actions. At first, it was bright with excitement. Then, her eyes shifted down Amelia's sweater toward her jeans as she said,

"Darling, is this what you wore to work today?" She said it so doubtfully.

"Of course not, Mom." Amelia stepped into the foyer, hugged her mother, then sauntered back toward the kitchen, where she found her father nibbling on an oatmeal cookie. She took one from the bowl, suddenly conscious that she hadn't bothered to eat anything that morning. The anxiety-vomit reflex was too strong.

"There she is. My little worker bee," her dad said with a smile.

"How are you doing, Dad?"

"Not bad," he said as he took another bite of raisin and oat. "Tell you the truth. I'm hankering to get out to see Olivia's new boutique hotel. There was a write-up in the paper about it today. I can't believe she hasn't asked us for more help. We only spent forty years as architects."

"I think Olivia and Anthony have their own vision for the place," Amelia said. She finished off her cookie and then surprised herself as she took another.

She could feel the judgmental eyes of her mother, the first woman who had ever taught her how to "diet" properly. What did she care, now? Nobody saw her, anyway.

"Still, it would have been polite of Olivia to ask," her father said.

"Amelia, I wanted to ask you something," her mother said, nearly speaking over her father. She shifted toward the oven and then drew out several pots and pans. On the counter sat a mass of various vegetables, tomatoes and onions, peppers and potatoes — all things Amelia and her mother would spend the next half-hour or so peeling and slicing.

Amelia sidled up next to her mother and washed her hands in

the sink as her mother placed two paring knives on the counter between them. "What's up?"

"Well, we happened to see Mandy last night," her mother said. "Your dad wanted to stop by to borrow Daniel's drill, and Mandy was on the couch when we came in. The girl looked absolutely listless, Amelia. I've never seen her like that before."

Amelia arched her eyebrow.

"I know how close you girls are," her mother continued. "And I wondered if maybe you know what's going on? I know she was running around with some boy for a while, but maybe he broke her heart? Oh, but really, she should be focused on what comes next. Hasn't she decided on a college? Isn't she making plans?"

Amelia lifted an onion from the pile of veggies and chopped off the stubby end. Immediately, the stench of it wafted over her eyes and tears sprung up.

"I think she's under a lot of pressure right now," Amelia said finally.

"Of course. But that's where we come in, isn't it?" her mother said.

"It does us no good to push her too far," Amelia offered.

"Oh, but these children, you sometimes have to push them," Anita offered as she scrubbed a red pepper beneath the sink. "I remember when you were a teenager. We never really had to guide you. You were always so driven. You always had a million plans. And look where it's taken you!"

Amelia grimaced.

"I just don't feel that Mandy has the same strength that you do."

"I don't think that's true at all," Amelia offered. She slid several finely-sliced pieces of onion into a large bowl and placed it off to the side, then dropped another onion onto the cutting board. Her heart performed a strange thud in her stomach.

"And I hate to say this, but I think she's gaining weight," her mother continued.

Amelia bristled and then chopped through another side of the onion. "I don't think that's true at all."

"When she stood up last night, I noticed it. Especially in her face," her mother continued. "And then, I watched her reach into the pantry and grab a huge box of Cheez-Its. She's going to have to learn that that teenage metabolism doesn't stick around for long."

Annoyed, Amelia stepped toward the bowl of cookies and took yet another — her third of the afternoon. Her mother's eyes flashed. Amelia could feel it: how much her mother wanted to scold her for over-eating sweets. But she held back.

"All we can do right now is support Mandy in all things," Amelia said, between bites of her oatmeal cookie. "I remember being a teenager. It was a rough time. And I'm sure it's gotten even stranger as the years have gone by."

"This social media stuff. It must rot their brains," Anita said with finality. "I just hope this is all only a memory by this time next year, when Mandy's off preparing to take over the world."

"I'm sure it will be," Amelia said, even as the truth crawled around in her stomach.

Mandy, Daniel, and Jake arrived for dinner just past five-thirty. Daniel grabbed a beer from the fridge and said, "I'm surprised you're already here! Don't you normally have meetings till six-thirty or seven?"

"Yep," Amelia said. "But not today."

"Our girl's been here since three!" Anita said.

"Wow," Daniel said. "Did the great and powerful Amelia Taylor finally learn how to take a break?"

"Something like that," Amelia said.

Mandy and Jake hovered on the other end of the counter. Amelia caught Mandy's eye for only a moment before Mandy dropped her gaze to the counter and reached for a cookie.

"You should wait till after dinner, honey," Anita said. "We've cooked up a big feast."

Mandy gave a light shrug. "I'm starving."

"The cookies are great," Amelia said. "Your grandpa and I have eaten our weight in them today."

"Ain't that the truth," Jason said.

Anita's eyes flashed from Amelia and back to Mandy, as though she wanted to reprimand both of them but wasn't quite sure how.

"Can you girls set the table for me?" Anita asked. "The chicken's almost ready."

Mandy and Amelia gathered up the plates and salad bowls, the forks, spoons, knives, and glasses, and headed out to the dining room, which Anita and Jason liked to use for special occasions and big family dinners. As Mandy placed a plate delicately at the head of the table, Amelia muttered under her breath.

"You doing okay today, Mandy?"

Mandy shrugged. "I tried to corner Colin to explain. But he told me he'd heard I was flirting with Paul, this football player, and that he didn't want anything to do with me anymore. He told me he was headed off to Yale, and he would try his best not to remember me."

Amelia's heart felt squeezed. "That's awful."

Mandy shrugged. "I should have known, I guess."

"But he still doesn't know. About the... You know."

"No," Mandy said. "But I can't figure out how to tell him about it, especially when he's so angry with me."

"Were you? Flirting with Paul, the football player?"

"Maybe. Probably. Paul's super cute, and I have to do something to keep my mind off of things."

Amelia nodded. This was something she understood — the personal distraction. Even now, this dinner with her family was something of a distraction from the horrors of her own life.

The family gathered around the table and dug into the meal: lemon chicken, mashed potatoes, gravy, a beautiful salad with bright spinach leaves in the base, speckled with blue cheese. In the distance, Anita played a Beethoven symphony on the speaker system, and for a while, the Taylor family was able to pretend that everything wasn't falling apart.

But very soon, Anita removed her talons and dug them directly into Mandy, yet again.

"You know, Mandy, I had a conversation with your friend Colin's grandmother recently."

Mandy's eyes filled with fire. It was almost impressive how horrible this topic of conversation was. Anita Taylor had really stepped in it.

"And apparently, he's off to Yale!" Anita said.

"He sure is," Mandy said. Her voice sizzled with sarcasm.

"Did you happen to apply to any Ivy League schools?" Anita asked.

Mandy shook her head. She then shoved her half-eaten plate forward and crossed her arms over her chest. "Nope."

"But you did apply to several good schools, didn't you?" Anita demanded. "Back when Amelia was looking into schools, she already had a pretty clear career trajectory ahead of her, so it didn't matter as much. But I know with kids your age, it's important to head out into the world and make something of yourself off the island. Don't you think so, Amelia?"

Amelia couldn't speak.

"Oh, Mandy, you really are so lucky to have your Aunt Amelia here for you through all this. She has such a sense of business. The people of this island trust her to get things done. Any question you have, you make sure to ask her. Isn't that right, Amelia?"

Mandy glared at her grandmother. Amelia's tongue turned to sandpaper. Jake, Grandpa Jason, and Daniel all seemed at a total loss of words. This was a battle between the women and the men knew better than to jump in.

Finally, Amelia spoke. "Actually, I don't know if I am the best person to speak to about this."

Anita's eyes twitched toward her. "What on earth are you talking about?"

"I've been forced to take a leave of absence, actually," Amelia blurted out suddenly. A strange grin snaked from ear-to-ear. "So I guess I wouldn't call myself the number-one employee of Martha's Vineyard. In a sense, I'm not an employee at all right now."

The air around the table shifted strangely. Amelia leaped to her feet, unable to make eye contact with her mother or even glance at Mandy. She then gathered her plate and headed to the kitchen, where she turned on the faucet and scrubbed her plate clean. Over the rush of the water, she could hear her mother's haggard whisper.

"What on earth happened to her! Daniel, do you know anything about this?"

"No, Mom. I think it must have just happened."

"What has happened to this family?" Anita demanded. "All Amelia's ever had is that job! How could she mess something up like this?"

Amelia's eyes welled. She turned up the faucet temperature as high as it would go until it scalded her fingers. She then dropped the plate into the drying rack, dried her hands, and stepped back toward the hallway. She could still make out the strange whispers from her mother at the dinner table.

At least she had taken the spotlight off Mandy, for now.

As Amelia reached for her coat, tears welled and rolled down her cheeks. She buttoned her coat to the top and then turned back toward the doorway, where Mandy stood, with her hand strapped across her stomach. Her eyes echoed back Amelia's sorrow. They'd both lost something major — their hope for their future.

"Thank you," Mandy breathed. "Thank you for getting her off of me."

Amelia stepped toward her niece and wrapped her in a hug. Her voice broke as she murmured, "You know I'd do anything for you, right?"

Mandy let out a single sob as Amelia stepped back. They held one another's gaze for a long time.

"I never needed her," Mandy said softly.

Amelia arched her brow. "What do you mean?"

"My mother. I never needed her. You were always more than enough. Thank you."

CHAPTER SIXTEEN

THE FOLLOWING AFTERNOON, Anita called Amelia several times, but Amelia refused to answer. She dropped the phone back on the couch and readjusted herself against the couch cushion. When her mother finally got the hint, she texted;

ANITA: You can't hide from me forever.

ANITA: I just want to talk to you.

ANITA: Help me understand what happened.

ANITA: Help me understand what went wrong.

But Amelia couldn't face it. Throughout her life, she had been nothing, if not perfect. Now, in the wake of her mother's clear judgment about her situation, she'd begun to wonder just why, all those years, she'd sought perfection. Had it brought her pleasure? Or had it all been for Anita and Jason Taylor, for their endless approval?

Amelia walked away from her phone as it buzzed with yet another message from Anita. Once in the kitchen, she opened the fridge for the twelfth time of the day, inspected the selection of yogurts and various low-fat cheeses, the vegetables that she needed to eat later to ensure they didn't rot and found that yet again, she wasn't hungry — just bored. This was a funny concept for her. Boredom had always been a thing she had heard about. In all honesty, she'd never believed in it.

Suddenly, Amelia's stomach stirred yet again. She walked into the bathroom and she stood, looking at her reflection in the mirror. There was something off about her complexion. Perhaps she needed to make a doctor's appointment. Perhaps it was finally time to head to a therapist and take a good, hard look at all that inner chaos between her ears.

There was a knock at the door. Amelia tied up her robe as she slipped back out toward the foyer. If she spotted her mother's vehicle in the driveway, she would think very hard about diving back between the sheets and ignoring her.

But there wasn't a car in the drive. Curious, Amelia snuck a peek out the window and caught sight of a backpack hanging off of a single shoulder of a terribly familiar girl. When she opened it, she found Mandy — dressed in jeans, a ratty t-shirt, and her long hair hanging in strings yet again. Her eyes echoed back sorrow.

The normal questions didn't come to Amelia immediately. She didn't ask Mandy why she wasn't in school, or why she hadn't showered, or where her father thought she was. Instead, she swung the door open wide and collected the poor girl in a hug. Together, they gathered under blankets in the living room, sipped hot cocoa, and waited for time to tick away. Time was Mandy's enemy, and Amelia knew that, but it was also the only barrier between them and the truth.

"I just couldn't face school today," Mandy said softly. "I couldn't face Colin or my friends who were whispering about me gaining weight or the teachers asking me why I'm not paying attention. I wish I could drop out."

Amelia rubbed Mandy's upper back as she began to cry. She wanted to tell her that one day, she'd discover that the friends who said stuff like that weren't actually friends at all. She wanted to say that one day she would find someone better than Colin, someone who treasured her for her heart, her soul and her kindness, rather than her beauty and school popularity.

Of course, Amelia never had. So she wasn't exactly in a position to be able to say something like that. She bit her lower lip nervously.

"I just keep thinking about what Dad will say," Mandy whispered. "He didn't ask me anything when we got home last night, although I know he wanted to. He talked about you, and about how you were always so perfect, and about how he's worried about you. But I could see it in his eyes. He's just as worried about me."

"Of course he is. It's kind of his job," Amelia said. "I'm a grown woman. I can take care of myself."

"I guess I am, too," Mandy whispered. "Or at least, I'm going to have to learn to be, very soon."

Their conversation faltered for a moment. Amelia rose to gather up some snacks for the two of them, which left Mandy to flick through the channels and then ultimately find a comedy on a streaming site.

"I can't even watch any romantic comedies these days," Mandy explained as she opened a bag of pretzels. "All that love feels like an attack."

"I know exactly what you mean," Amelia said. "As all my friends got married and had babies, I just felt myself growing in my career. Every step forward felt monumental for me. And now, well."

"They'll let you come back," Mandy offered. "They have to. You basically keep that place running."

That moment, there was another knock at the door. Amelia checked her phone to find even more unanswered calls and messages from her mother, and her heart swelled with panic. Perhaps she'd finally made her way there, only to discover Amelia and Mandy both playing hooky from their lives.

But when Amelia opened the door, she found herself face-to-face with one of her greatest enemies.

The man who'd ruined her life stood on her doorstep, dressed in an Italian-cut suit, which had certainly cost him a pretty penny; his hair was windswept and gorgeous, as though he'd literally just stepped off his sailboat, and his green eyes caught the soft light of the mid-afternoon.

"Mr. Krispin," Amelia said, careful to make her voice hard and unwelcoming.

"Amelia," Oliver returned. He said her name as though it was music.

In fact, Amelia had never heard someone say her name the way he did.

She crossed her arms over her chest, suddenly conscious that she wore no bra and had only a pair of shorts and a white t-shirt on under her pink robe.

"Can I help you?" Amelia demanded. "As you can see, I'm incredibly busy."

Oliver gave her the slightest of smiles. From the living room came the opening credits of the film Mandy had picked, a comedy with Will Ferrell — basically the opposite of "work."

"Yeah. You seem really busy," Oliver returned.

"Glad you stopped by to insult me," Amelia said. "I really appreciate you taking time out of your schedule."

Hurriedly, Amelia reached up and began to push the door closed. But Oliver placed a hand against the wood and steadied it. Her eyes caught his, and again, her heart dropped into her stomach.

"Listen. Amelia," Oliver said.

"You told me you were headed off the island. You told me you were going to build somewhere else."

"I don't want to build anywhere else," Oliver said. "I told you. I love Martha's Vineyard. I want to be a part of this island."

"You already have so many other properties," Amelia interjected.

"I know that. Of course, I know that. But Zane called me back. He said it would benefit the island to have the resort. I was overjoyed. I thought maybe you'd had a change of heart and were willing to help me with the permits."

Amelia's nostrils flared. "Not quite."

"I understand that now." Oliver's shoulders dropped forward. "I can't believe he demanded that you take a leave of absence."

Amelia shrugged. "I guess that's just what happens when you care about something too much. You get screwed for it. I should have known, really. I got too comfortable."

Oliver turned his eyes toward the ground as though her words had actually injured him. Was it possible to actually hurt someone like Oliver Krispin's feelings? Couldn't he just make anything happen, make anyone say any compliment to him, with just the wave of his credit card?

"I feel awful about this," Oliver said.

Amelia shrugged. "Don't. It's a waste of your time."

Oliver paused for a long moment. Again, Amelia toyed with slamming the door in his face.

"Let me take you out to dinner," he said.

Amelia chortled. "No. Why would I want to go out to dinner with you?"

"Come on. I owe it to you, after everything that's happened."

"You don't owe me anything," Amelia returned flatly. "I just want to be left alone."

Oliver palmed the back of his neck. "I might be the only person on the planet who can help get you back to work, you know."

Amelia's lips parted in shock. "That sounds like some kind of threat."

"It's not meant to be one," Oliver said. "I just think we should create a strategy. Maybe there's a way that both of us can have what we want."

Amelia resented him more than ever. He stood there on her front stoop, terrifically handsome, with his project green-lit and assuredly millions headed his way. Beyond all that, he was right: he was probably the only one who could talk any reason past Zane's thick skull.

"A business dinner," Amelia said firmly. She then lifted her hand out to shake his. His grip was sturdy. It seemed to evoke his respect for her.

"Does tomorrow work for you?" he asked.

"Okay." Amelia dropped her hands to her sides, then asked, "Should I wear this robe or another one?"

Oliver laughed aloud. Amelia was surprised that she'd even mustered the strength for a joke around this horrendous man.

"This one will do just fine," Oliver said as he stepped back from the door. "You can store your own hot sauce in the oversized pockets."

"Very good point," Amelia said as she snuck her hands into those very pockets now. They were lined with wrappers and kleenex. She was grateful he couldn't see.

"I'll see you tomorrow then, Amelia," Oliver said. "I'll pick you up at seven. I look forward to it."

CHAPTER SEVENTEEN

"IT'S NOT A DATE." Amelia flung several different outfits across her bed as she repeated these words to Jennifer. She'd said the words to herself over and over again throughout the morning. Now, as she tried out the words on Jennifer, her voice wavered slightly, as though she didn't fully believe them.

"Sure. Of course not," Jennifer said. "It's just a business meeting that you want to look super-hot for."

"Exactly," Amelia said. "I want to beat him in as many ways as I can."

"But what's the idea here, exactly?" Jennifer asked as she lifted one of the blouses from the bed and analyzed the stitching across the top of the collar. Anita Taylor had sewn it herself for Amelia's Christmas present a few years before.

"The idea?"

"Yeah. Like, do you want your job back so that you can work on this resort again? Or do you want your job back so you can get Oliver Krispin off the island? What?"

Amelia struggled with the question. "I don't want him to build on that land. I'll do anything to stop it, actually."

"But what if that means you can't keep your job?" Jennifer asked.

Amelia buzzed her lips. "I have no idea."

"It's a Catch-22, isn't it." Jennifer walked toward the side of the room, where she inspected Amelia's various high-heels. "But you're right. It's never a bad thing to look hot. Even on a non-date."

"That's why you're here. I need the Jennifer Conrad approval."

Jennifer tapped her nose as she inspected the various elements strewn across the bed and lined up on the floor. "I think the short black shirt, the blouse Anita made, the black jacket, and the Bottega Venetta pointed-toe heels."

"You're the master," Amelia said. "All I know these days is slippers and robe."

"Slippers and robe are about to have a huge season," Jennifer teased. "You're really ahead of your time."

"Fashion-forward, some might say," Amelia said with a laugh.

Jennifer headed out a bit later, as she had lunch with her son, followed by a meeting at her social media company downtown.

"It's kind of nice to be away from the bakery today," Jennifer said as she donned her white spring jacket and flipped her red hair over her shoulders. "I don't reek of coffee and donuts. And I talked to Mom about maybe hiring another staff member. As much as I love the Frosted Delights, it's not really my calling, the way it always was Mom's. You know?"

"You need a break," Amelia affirmed. "Although I can tell you.

Now that I have more time off than I've ever had in my entire life, I don't know quite what to do with myself. I feel like a bump on a log."

OLIVER ARRIVED AT SEVEN, just as he'd said he would. He was the dependable sort. Amelia had to give him that. Just before he rang the doorbell, Amelia opened the door and stepped out into the fresh spring air. His eyes opened just the slightest bit wider, proof that the way she'd dressed was noticed and appreciated. Mission accomplished. If she could get her job back and reject him all at once, she would feel on top of the world.

"Hey there," Oliver said.

"Hey yourself."

"Do you want to grab your robe? Just in case you get cold."

"I think I can manage without," Amelia returned.

Oliver's car suited his brand, of course. It was a swanky-looking vintage Mercedes, charcoal, and it had probably cost upwards of a million, maybe more. To men like Oliver, that was pocket change. He opened the passenger door for her and Amelia slid onto the leather seats and then folded her hands over her lap. She tried to make a deal with her heart to stop its wild, anxious beating. She hoped he couldn't sense how strangely nervous she was.

"So. Where are we off to for our business meeting?" Amelia asked as he turned the key in the ignition. It felt exhilarating to be so close to him, with his hand on the stick just a few inches left of her knee. Maybe in another reality, she might have imagined or pined for his hand ticking over and wrapping around her thigh.

"I thought we'd head to The Terrace," he said.

Amelia's lips parted in shock. The Terrace, which was connected to the Charlotte Inn, was one of the most expensive and swankiest restaurants in all of Edgartown. She'd only been there once for Daniel and Suzy's rehearsal dinner. For this reason, she'd always felt a darkness around the restaurant. To her, it was a symbol of bad luck.

In any case, she had never imagined that she'd ever had a scenario in which she'd be asked out to dinner there.

"I see," she said as his beautiful car churned out onto Peases Point Way.

"You sound less than enthused." Oliver's eyes flashed. "It was recommended to me by an old colleague of mine. I think you might know him. His girlfriend's name is Jennifer Conrad."

Amelia wanted to blurt out what she'd learned from Jennifer — that Derek wasn't so keen on Oliver. But she wasn't in any position to make him mad.

"The Terrace is one of the better restaurants on Martha's Vineyard," she said finally. "And certainly, it's one of the most expensive. I suppose that's what you look for first."

"I like to experience the finer things in life, it's true," Oliver offered. "I don't think that's necessarily a bad thing. Do you?"

Amelia decided not to answer. She turned her head to gaze out the window. On the corner, she spotted Lola Sheridan and her boyfriend, Tommy Gasbarro, hand-in-hand, waiting for the light to change. On the far end of the next block, Stan Ellis, who was Tommy Gasbarro's ex-step-father, waved a hand. If Amelia remembered correctly, Lola Sheridan's mother, Anna, had had an affair with Stan Ellis years before. He'd been there when she'd died in that horrible accident.

Amelia still remembered that strange, fateful night. Back then, Michelle had still been alive, and tragedy hadn't been so close to home.

"I've rented a house along the water," Oliver said then. "Beautiful place, fully furnished. It even comes with a baby grand piano."

Amelia wondered if he said these things as a way to impress her. She wanted to point out how little she cared about money. It wasn't like she was poor or anything; she was comfortable. But more than that, she'd never made a single decision in her life that was all about money. Her decisions were rooted in family and love and the island's beauty. She wasn't driven by profit.

Unlike men like Oliver Krispin.

Oliver parked the Mercedes. As she stepped out onto the sidewalk, Oliver rushed around the back and said, "I planned to open the door for you. Like a gentleman does."

"No need," Amelia said coldly. "I've managed to open plenty of doors on my own over the years."

"Maybe you should give lessons," Oliver returned.

The joke again surprised her. Amelia let out a single laugh and then tried to swallow it back. Oliver gave her a look that told her just how clever and funny and interesting he thought he was. Her eyebrows lowered. She had to keep it together.

They appeared at the front of the restaurant, where the hostess greeted them warmly. Amelia eyed the diners and realized that, for maybe the first time in a long time, she didn't recognize a single person. This wasn't your typical islander's night out joint.

"Oliver Krispin. For two," Oliver said.

The hostess eyed Amelia. Amelia wondered what the look meant. Did she perhaps think Amelia wasn't good-looking enough for this handsome and clearly rich man? Was she asking herself, why her?

"Right this way," the hostess said. She turned and swung her hips to-and-fro as they walked through the tables, which flickered with the soft light from the candles. They marched all the way to the back, where the hostess opened up a little side door and led them into a private room, with gorgeous, vintage-looking wallpaper, and a single, long table, set with china.

Oliver pulled out a chair for Amelia as Amelia peered at him curiously. "What is this?"

Oliver flashed another arrogant smile. "This is where we're dining."

"But—" But before Amelia could protest, the hostess stepped up alongside them and began to describe some of the expensive wines they currently served, along with the day's menu, which constantly changed. Oliver sat across from Amelia and then gestured for Amelia to sit, as though he had to remind her not to be rude.

Amelia just felt like a fish out of water.

"I think the '98 Merlot will suit us just fine," Oliver said evenly. "Along with some roasted garlic for now."

The waitress bowed her head and retreated back into the beautiful restaurant. She pulled the door closed behind her, which meant it was just Amelia and Oliver, Oliver and Amelia, in a space from the rest of society.

"Why won't you sit down?" Oliver said finally, after a strange, tense moment of silence.

How could Amelia explain? He looked at her now as though she had three heads. Slowly, she gripped her chair and dragged it out, then sat.

"I just don't understand why we have to be all cooped up in here," Amelia said finally.

"It's what I always do with business meetings," Oliver returned. "And you said it was a business meeting, didn't you?"

"Yes." Amelia's heart pattered quickly. Was she just nervous about being so close to him? "We're just so far from everyone else. It feels weird to be at a restaurant, without all the ambiance."

"Really?" Oliver continued to blink at her as though he hardly recognized her. "I normally get so annoyed at everyone around me. You can hear every boring and banal conversation."

"Are you suggesting that the people on Martha's Vineyard are too boring and banal for you to sit close to?"

Oliver arched his eyebrow. "I think you're trying to look for reasons to be mad when there aren't any."

"Is that so?" Amelia demanded. She felt a sudden rush of energy, as though every moment thus far since she'd taken her leave of absence had built toward this one.

At that moment, the waitress arrived back with their wine. She tilted the bottle toward Oliver, who nodded, then watched as she removed the cork, then poured the tiniest bit of liquid into his large glass. He lifted the glass so that two fingers sat on either side of the stem, and then he sipped. His gentle nod told the woman to pour them both glasses. Amelia wondered if she sensed the tension between them.

When the waitress left, Oliver lifted his glass of wine toward Amelia. Amelia crossed her arms over her chest, suddenly disgusted with all of this. *Why had she come here with this man? Did he really plan to help her get back to work, or did he want to toy with her like this — take her out for strange private dinners and make fun of her?*

"To you," he said. He then waited for Amelia to lift her glass, but she made no motion to.

"I don't feel up to drinking," Amelia said.

Annoyance fluttered through Oliver's eyes. He cleared his throat and then took a big sip of wine. "Okay. It's only four hundred dollars a bottle. But okay."

"Enjoy," Amelia returned as she flashed him a huge smile.

What did he care if he spent four hundred dollars? He was made of money.

"So. Tell me. What's up with Zane?" Amelia said somberly.

"Don't you want to order food before we get started on business?"

"No. I want to get started as soon as possible."

"Hmm. Well. Then." He returned the menu to the tablecloth and lifted his wine glass again. "You should know that he's started calling you a 'previous' employee."

Amelia's blood ran cold. She gripped the fabric of her skirt hard, as though she wanted to restrain herself. "You don't even know all the trouble I've gone through to keep that place above water."

Oliver shrugged. "Let me ask you this, Amelia. Didn't you ever want to do anything else? I mean, you seem like a smart woman. Much smarter than Zane or any of those other clowns down at city hall."

Amelia's chin quivered. "I don't know if that's a compliment or some kind of insult."

Oliver chuckled. "Take it however you want. I can already tell; you're winding yourself up."

Amelia shot up from the chair. She glared at him and then demanded of herself why, why, why she remained in that stupid, closed-off room with this man. Before she knew what she was doing, she shot through the door and headed back toward the foyer of the fancy restaurant. When she reached the sidewalk, she began to walk away from the restaurant, as her eyes became wet with sorrow and anger.

"Amelia! Hey!"

Oliver wasn't far behind her. She clacked forward, her arms crossed over her chest and her eyes focused on the western horizon. She prayed for one of her best friends to drive by if only so she could make a quick escape.

But seconds later, there was the sound of racing feet, and Oliver's hand clasped around her elbow to make her stop. "Amelia! Stop, will you?"

Amelia yanked herself around and glared at this rich specimen. "I'm sorry. Did you want something from me? Or did you just want to rub in all this power you have over my job and my position on the island and the people of the island and the island itself?"

Oliver seemed disheartened. It was clear that the evening hadn't gone in the direction he'd wanted it to.

"Just come back inside, Amelia. Please. I want to buy you dinner. I promised I would."

Amelia drew her elbow away from his hand. "I'm not hungry."

"Perfect. We can order those ridiculously expensive small plates. It's barely food, anyway," Oliver said.

Amelia's chin quivered. She couldn't snap out of her anger and sadness. "You really don't know what you've taken from me, do you? You don't understand that none of this is really a joke to me."

A car whipped past; its tires slashed through a puddle and splattered the dark water across the sidewalk. Amelia turned her eyes toward the puddles.

"I really do want to help you," Oliver said finally. "It's the reason we're here together."

"You don't understand," Amelia said softly. "People don't help me. I've never needed help. I'm the one who helps. I'm there for everyone. It's my—my thing. It's—"

Just then, her stomach gurgled so loud that Amelia stopped speaking. She turned her eyes toward her belly. Her body had totally betrayed her.

And at that moment, Oliver laughed aloud. Amelia's giggle rolled out a few seconds after that. The two of them stood out there in the grey darkness of early spring, laughing themselves silly. If asked about it later, Amelia wouldn't have been able to say what the heck was so funny. But in these moments, she felt strangely united with this man, as though he was someone she'd known a long time.

"I think it's possible I'm just really hungry," Amelia said as she clenched her eyes tight. "And I don't think I can be blamed for anything I say."

"I'm starving, too," Oliver admitted.

Amelia turned back toward the restaurant. She could still practically see that long-ago evening when she and Suzy and

Daniel had gathered outside before the rehearsal dinner. The place seemed cursed.

"Do you mind if we go somewhere else?" she finally asked.

Oliver laughed again. "I swear. No other woman on the planet would make a fuss about the special night I just planned."

"I just can't go back in there," Amelia said. "And those small plates? I don't think they're going to cut it."

Oliver brushed a strand of hair from his forehead and gave her a tender smile. "Where do you want to go?"

CHAPTER EIGHTEEN

AMELIA AND OLIVER stood in front of the Edgartown diner, a place Amelia and her best friends had frequented as teenagers — with glowing white tables and retro furnishings and a jukebox in the corner. Oliver's eyes were doubtful, and Amelia slipped her arm through his and said, "It's the best of the best of all the comfort foods. Fries. Onion rings. Grilled cheese sandwiches. Chicken tenders."

Oliver rolled his eyes playfully. "You know, The Terrace had a special on snails tonight. I couldn't wait to show you. They cook them in this garlic sauce, and—"

"I'm sorry, what was that?" Amelia said as she rushed forward and pressed the door open. "Something about mozzarella sticks?"

Once in the diner, Amelia had to admit that Oliver looked entirely out of place. Not a single soul, in the history of the diner, had worn such a spectacular suit within its walls, and the various diner regulars looked up at him as though he'd stepped out of the pages of a magazine. Oliver blushed, as though, for the first time in a long time, he realized his money mattered very little.

To Amelia's surprise, Chelsea, Olivia's daughter, was at work. She'd broken her leg in a freak accident at Olivia's inherited mansion the previous month, but she sped around easily on crutches and ordered her boyfriend, Xavier, to take various plates and trays out to customers. They had quite a formula worked out, one that seemed seamless so that all the orders were delivered on time, and all the tips were pocketed by the two of them. Amelia could feel the new yet hopeful love that brewed between them. Olivia had mentioned that Xavier and Chelsea planned to leave the island together in the near future. Probably, they'd already begun to save up.

Chelsea eased over her crutches clacking and her smile widening. "Amelia!" she said. "I haven't seen you in a while."

"You look fantastic, Chels," Amelia said. "You whip around here faster on crutches than I do on two legs."

"I've really mastered them. Maybe I'll even miss them when they take the cast off. I'm just glad they let me come back. I was getting so bratty sitting on the couch all the time. I think we watched every single movie that has ever been made. Xavier was about to lose his mind."

Chelsea's eyes turned toward Oliver, who looked increasingly anxious, as though for the first time ever, he had no idea what to say.

"Anyway. You two look like you're headed to the symphony or something," Chelsea said. She slipped a pen behind her ear and leaned heavily on her crutches.

"Actually, we're just here for dinner," Amelia said.

"Huh. Okay. Well. I have this table by the window free. Does that work?"

Amelia and Oliver sat across from one another in strange silence as Chelsea smacked two laminated menus between them and then cut back toward the kitchen. In the meantime, Xavier arrived with two ice waters. "Chelsea will be by to get your orders in a sec," he announced before he headed back in her direction. Just before Amelia looked away, he placed a hand on the base of Chelsea's back and whispered something in her ear. Amelia could feel it — the hope between them.

"So, what do you think of the menu?" Amelia asked finally.

Oliver cleared his throat. "It certainly doesn't align with my nutritional values."

Amelia laughed aloud. "Nutritional values?"

"You know, low carb, high protein—that kind of thing."

"Right. It sounds like you really know how to live," Amelia said.

Oliver blushed and placed his menu off to the side. He then folded his hands over the table and wagged his eyebrows.

"What is that look for?" Amelia asked.

"It means I'm ready to order."

"The salad, no dressing?"

"Something like that," Oliver said.

Chelsea arrived back and blinked down at them, her pen poised on her notepad. "Ready when you are."

"Okay. Great. I'll have the grilled cheese with a side of onion rings," Amelia said. "Plus, hmm. A diet coke."

Chelsea jotted down various notes and then turned her eyes toward Oliver. Her expression was lined with doubt.

"And for you?"

Oliver cleared his throat. His eyes glittered strangely.

"This is my first time here," he began. "So I want to make sure I get to taste all of your cuisines. I'd like to start with breadsticks, with both garlic and cheese dipping sauce, along with mozzarella sticks and a side of pickle rings."

Amelia's jaw dropped.

"After that, for my main course, I'd like the double-cheeseburger with bacon and, of course, french fries. It seems like this is the type of place where you have to try the fries. Right?"

Chelsea nodded. "Yeah. They're killer."

"Great. And I want a milkshake. Chocolate. But bring out a strawberry milkshake too, for the lady."

Amelia forced her eyes to meet Oliver's. Chelsea made a final note and then said, "I'll bring a wheelbarrow out after to take you out of the restaurant."

"Great service." Oliver winked. He wore a grin from ear to ear.

Chelsea gathered the menus as Amelia continued to sit in shock. After a long pause, she clucked her tongue and said, "You really know how to order."

Oliver shrugged. "I can't just come in here and get a run-of-the-mill burger. I want to experience this diner in all its greasy glory. And! I want to do it while listening to something good." Oliver grabbed his wallet and found three dollar bills, which he then took over to the jukebox.

Amelia watched him, totally mesmerized, as he flipped through the CDs from other eras and typed in the numbers to his chosen songs. By the time he arrived back, Fleetwood Mac's "Everywhere" flourished from the speakers.

"I love this song," Amelia said, totally surprised that he'd picked something so close to her heart.

"Me too," he said.

Xavier arrived with the breadsticks and the mozzarella sticks. Oliver grabbed a breadstick, tore it in half, and dunked the doughy part into the garlic. As he did it, he said, "I've already given up on trying to kiss you, so I guess garlic it is."

Amelia laughed aloud again. She grabbed the other half of his breadstick and followed his lead. "I told you. This is a business meeting."

"Yeah. It really feels like that." Oliver's words sizzled with sarcasm, but they weren't unkind.

After a long moment of silence, Oliver swallowed his breadstick and then added, "I really haven't eaten anything this delicious in a long time. It makes five-star New York cuisine look sad."

"Long live the diner," Amelia said. "I have so many memories in this place."

"So many guys, I guess," Oliver returned. "You probably bring us all here."

Amelia's cheeks burned. Delicately, she placed the second half of her mozzarella stick on her plate and dried her hands of grease. "Actually, not really. To be honest with you, I haven't done much dating over the years. My life was my job. And now, I don't have anything. Weird to say, I know. But it's true."

Oliver chewed contemplatively. "It's not weird to say. I'm kind of a workaholic myself. I respect that kind of life."

Amelia nodded. "I am grateful that I found a career that fulfills me so much. I know it's not a common thing."

"Right."

"But, well. I can't help but think that I've really neglected some major parts of what life is meant to be," Amelia continued.

Why was she speaking so openly? Was it the grease on her tongue? Was it the Fleetwood Mac on the speakers? There was something strange and outside of time here.

"Like, a few weeks ago, I went on a date with a guy I met after he hit my car," Amelia continued.

Oliver's eyes sparkled. "Wow. That's a funny way to meet someone."

"Yep. I thought so, too, until I went out on the date and realized I had absolutely no idea what to say to this guy. I felt like a complete idiot. He was kind of like you, very wealthy and powerful. He had the world on a string, that kind of thing. And then, to make matters worse, I went back to his hotel room and had to do the walk of shame back to my car," Amelia said.

Oliver laughed appreciatively. Amelia was surprised that he didn't make her feel like a loser with three heads.

"A walk of shame. Haven't done that in a while," Oliver returned.

"Can men even do a walk of shame? I thought that was a purely woman-only action."

"Sure. We can feel shame as we walk," Oliver said with a laugh. "Women don't have a moratorium on walks of shame."

"Learn something new every day," Amelia said.

The rest of their food arrived, along with the milkshakes. Amelia sucked at her strawberry shake greedily and immediately got a brain freeze. Oliver laughed aloud as another of his songs came on the jukebox — Bruce Springsteen's "Dancing In The Dark."

"Man. You're making it almost impossible not to get up and start dancing," Amelia said.

"That was the plan," Oliver said. "Get Amelia up on the table to give us a real show."

Amelia giggled and then took a small bite of her perfectly crisp grilled cheese. She moaned and then placed her hand over her mouth, embarrassed at the sound. But Oliver joined her in his moaning as he chewed his double-cheeseburger with bacon.

"This is what living is, apparently," Oliver stated. "Close down all the expensive restaurants. Return all your high-fashion clothing. It's sweatpants and onion rings from here on out."

As the minutes ticked past, Amelia was amazed at how familiar Oliver became to her. She felt totally comfortable, so much so that she finally said, "Tell me something about you that has nothing to do with your career."

Olivier dried his hands of grease and considered her words. Next, the jukebox played a song from Jim Croce, which was tender and sweet and terribly sad.

"I used to be married," he said finally.

Amelia's heart dropped just the slightest bit. Here, she'd thought he was this hard-edged, brash, arrogant individual, incapable of love. How wrong she'd been.

"She was my life. We met on the first day of college, and I asked her to marry me only a year later. We were just kids. Slowly, I built up my career, and she was happy to come along with me. We moved to New York, and we built up a little plan for ourselves. Enjoy our mid-twenties, and then get serious about having a family."

Amelia couldn't breathe. Everything he said felt tremendously heavy.

"Anyway, when that time came, we started to struggle," Oliver continued. "No babies came. And so we went to the doctor, and he did some tests on both of us. It turns out — it was me. I was shooting blanks. All those years of birth control and I'd been shooting blanks."

Amelia dropped her eyes to the table. "I'm so sorry."

He shrugged and took a bite of a French fry. "We were pretty devastated. This had been our plan, and then, nature got in the way. We started to talk about other options, but my career started to really take off after that, and I soon found that we didn't talk about anything at all. Not well, anyway. It was kind of like we were strangers. And then, one day, she told me she was pregnant."

"What?" Amelia whispered.

"Yeah. At first, I was overjoyed. Like, finally. Something had gone our way. But then she burst into tears and said it wasn't mine. That all she had wanted the past few years was a baby of her own. She left me and moved in with him, and after that, well. I burrowed myself deeper and deeper into my work."

Oliver rubbed his palms together as his cheeks flushed pink. "And now, I guess, I've just given you all the gritty details of my personal life—at a diner."

"No better place to put it all out there," Amelia said. "Diners are the backbone of America." She swallowed a bit of strawberry milkshake and then added, "I'm just so sorry all of that happened. It sounds really rough."

"It's been years, now," Oliver said. "Sometimes, when I think about the story, it sounds like it was a part of someone else's life."

"I think I know what you mean."

They held one another's gaze for a long moment. Amelia's heart felt on the verge of shattering.

"Listen. Amelia," Oliver said. "Tomorrow, we have a meeting scheduled for the resort."

Amelia had very nearly forgotten what all this was actually about.

"I see."

"I really want you there," Oliver said softly. "Zane doesn't know what he's talking about. And after all you've told me about this island, I just want to make sure everything we do is up to code and legal and respectful of the Vineyard and all its residents."

Amelia's throat tightened with emotion. "I don't know if I'm allowed to be there, Oliver."

"I'm the developer. What I say goes," Oliver said somberly.

CHAPTER NINETEEN

AMELIA REMAINED awake throughout the night for a number of reasons. One, she wanted to go through every single permit, every single law and rule, and all the plans that Oliver had for the resort to create a kind of plan moving forward, one that honored the island and the natural world she so cherished. But secondly, she supposed she couldn't have slept if she'd tried. Her night with Oliver made her mind and her heart and her stomach quake. She wasn't sure if she was afraid or overjoyed or something of both. Even still, when she tried to put herself to bed around three-thirty in the morning, all she could do was blink into the black above her bed and imagine what it might be like to kiss him. She hadn't had a proper crush in years. She knew this one would fade, just as all the other ones had. Still, it was kind of fun to feel not-so-dead inside for a change.

The following morning, Amelia drove her familiar route toward city hall. Unlike other mornings, she didn't park in her designated parking spot, as someone else had planted their vehicle directly between the lines. She glared at it as she walked up, annoyed. It was just a parking spot, but it had meant a lot to her over the years. This, maybe, was pathetic, too.

When she entered, her secretary, Clara ogled her strangely and then hissed, "What are you doing here!" Excitement poured out from her as she hustled over to Amelia to give her a discrete hug.

"I have a meeting with Mr. Krispin and Zane," Amelia replied.

"I don't have you down as a member of the meeting," Clara said, her eyebrows lowered.

"Oliver requested I attend," Amelia said. "I stayed up all night making a presentation."

"Of course you did," her secretary returned. "I always told you to try to get more rest. Glad to hear you're still ignoring my advice."

Warmed and terribly grateful, Amelia stepped toward the boardroom and then entered without a sound. Zane was in the midst of telling Oliver a story, and he hardly glanced her way.

"That was back when whaling was a big part of the island's industry," Zane continued.

"I see," Oliver returned. "This island sure has a lot of history. I've heard tell of the deaf community here and how they had a particular kind of Martha's Vineyard sign language."

Zane balked at him. "I see you've done some reading about our island?"

Oliver's eyes turned toward Amelia. This forced Zane to yank his head around. Silence blanketed the room.

"Amelia. What are you doing here?" Zane demanded.

"I requested that she attend," Oliver affirmed.

Zane looked flustered, as though he was out in the rain without an umbrella. "But Mr. Krispin, we've discussed everything. I told you. I took her off the project."

"And I believe she's the best person for the job," Oliver returned. "I've worked in this industry a long time, and I've never come across someone more knowledgeable. It's clear we would be remiss to eliminate her."

Zane's eyes were like daggers. Amelia shifted her weight, still unable to sit at the table with them.

"I really don't feel comfortable about you going behind my back like this," Zane offered.

At this, Amelia interjected. "I've prepared a presentation that outlines a plan I have to ensure the resort honors the land and history of Martha's Vineyard. I've expressed this importance to Mr. Krispin and he agrees that he wants to uphold everything the island holds dear. Yes, this means more time and it may mean that we can't open up in time for the end of the tourist season. But if we don't honor our island and its history and its nature, then what kind of beasts are we? Can we really give everything over for money?"

Zane balked again. He gave Oliver a horrible, red-eyed look and said, "We discussed the benefit of what an early opening would have for the island. I thought we agreed."

Oliver shook his head. "I had time to think, and I've come to the conclusion that Ms. Taylor is correct."

Zane looked stuck. He folded and unfolded his hands, furrowed his brow, then glared out the window. Amelia imagined that he'd already explained the situation to a number of high-rollers on the island; probably, they had called him their champion for opening the place so early and bringing in such revenue. This was a hindrance to all of that. It bruised his ego.

"I suppose, if you demand Ms. Taylor work on the project, I can't do anything to stand in the way of that," Zane finally said.

Oliver's eyes found Amelia's as a shiver raced up and down her spine. After a long pause, Amelia lifted her folder again and said, "Very well. I don't want to waste any more time. Let's have a look at my presentation, shall we? I really did spend all night making it."

***

AFTER THE MEETING, Zane followed Amelia back to her office. Amelia felt his presence like a ghost behind her. He clipped the door closed as she sauntered around the side of her desk. She really could have jumped up on the desk and danced across it. She was terribly pleased.

"I want you to know that I'll be watching you like a hawk," Zane warned as she slapped her folder across the desk and blinked up at him. "If you march out of line again, or make decisions outside of your jurisdiction, then I will not hesitate to take you out of your role again. Maybe I can't take you off this project with Mr. Krispin, as he's apparently taken some kind of liking to you, but I can certainly say you're unfit for any projects down the line."

Amelia couldn't drop from cloud nine. She nodded, smiled, and said, "Thanks for taking me back, boss."

The slight sarcasm clearly infuriated him, but there was nothing more to be said. He nodded, gripped the doorknob, and said, "Well then. I—hmm." He seemed to be caught between many ideas at once. "If you could please look at your previous calendar. I may need your assistance tomorrow at a number of meetings."

Amelia sensed it. He wanted to grovel and ask for assistance. If she had to guess, things had been a mess around there since her leave of absence.

"I'll check it out," Amelia offered. "If I'm not too busy with the Krispin project, I'll swing by."

Zane nodded. Shame made his shoulders curve forward. "Thank you." He disappeared through the door after that but left it cracked open enough for Amelia's secretary to peek her head through.

"Are you seriously back?" she cried as she stepped in and whipped the door closed.

Amelia nodded as tears brewed in her eyes. Clara rushed toward her, wrapped her arms around her, and squealed. "Oh my, gosh! It's been awful here without you!" she cried. "I can't even tell you. Zane has given me way too many responsibilities, and nobody seems to have their head screwed on right. With you back, everything can go back to normal."

"I can honestly say I was a bit lost without this place, too," Amelia said with a light shrug.

"Let me get you something," her secretary said brightly. "Something delicious for lunch. A salad? A burger? A wrap? Anything. Even if it's across the island, I'll drive there and pick it up for you."

Amelia's stomach clenched tightly. She wasn't sure if she was hungry or nervous, or a little of both. "Nothing, for now, thanks," she said. "But I'll let you know if I need anything."

Her secretary left her be after that. The moment the door

closed and Amelia found herself again alone in the office she'd so loved for many years, she turned, fell into her chair and watched as her hands shook.

Her nerves were a wreck and her anxiety was at an all-time high considering the circumstances. After she took a few deep breaths, she composed an email to a nearby therapy office. It was finally time to do something about the inner chaos of her mind.

CHAPTER TWENTY

AFTER SEVERAL WEEKS FLEW PAST, it was now April. Sunlight shimmered through the curtains of Amelia's office as she puttered through another conversation with yet another contractor. Things were coming together for Oliver and his resort; permits were filled out correctly; time was set aside to ensure everything was done properly. And all the while, Amelia felt hyper-focused on her career, grateful to have a purpose when she awoke every day.

"That sounds good to me," Amelia stated, as the contractor suggested a meeting the following morning at ten. "I'll see you then, Paul."

Amelia jotted several notes to herself on her desk and then aligned her post-it notes in order of importance. It was nearly four-thirty, and she longed to step out into the beautiful afternoon, if only for a few minutes, until she returned to her computer to finalize the rest of her daily tasks.

That moment, there was a knock at the door. After Amelia

called, "Come in," Mandy appeared in the doorway. She wore a pair of sweats, and her hair was all knotted up on top of her head. She looked defeated, as though she'd spent most of her day crying. And in a moment, Amelia swallowed her up in a hug and allowed the poor girl to drape her head on her forehead and shake.

"Let me call off my meetings the rest of the day," Amelia said suddenly.

Mandy lifted her blotchy face. "You don't have to do that."

"I insist," Amelia said. "When was the last time we went hiking at Felix Neck? I think this day calls for it."

Amelia gathered her things and led Mandy out to her parking spot, which had been dutifully passed back over to her upon her arrival back to her position. They then drove toward Peases Point Way, where Amelia changed clothes, grabbed a few snacks, and donned her tennis shoes. Within the half-hour, they ducked out of her car and snuck into the trees, where the light filtered through the sudden green buds, and that beautiful, damp smell of spring ballooned around them.

They didn't speak for a while. Amelia felt she had to let Mandy create the rhythm. It was easy for Amelia to say that time passed swiftly, that she couldn't very well wait a full nine months to tell her father the news. But basic facts had nothing at all to do with the emotional toll of being a senior in high school and pregnant.

"I'm sorry that I canceled that doctor's appointment," Mandy said suddenly.

They'd already discussed it. They had planned to head together to the doctor's appointment the following week. It was essential for the health of the baby.

"I wish you wouldn't have done that," Amelia murmured.

"I just don't know how to face it."

"I understand that. But you have to. It's for both you and the baby," Amelia said.

Mandy stopped walking and splayed her hand across her stomach. She then lifted her chin so that it pointed at the bright blue sky between the tree-tops. "Everything hurts when you're pregnant. My boobs are killing me. And I throw up all the time, Aunt Amelia. I'm always in that stupid high school bathroom, trying to hide how sick I am. I can't focus on anything because my brains have turned to mush."

Something in the back of Amelia's mind shifted. She turned her own chin toward the blue sky and watched as a long-necked bird swept over the treetops. As she stood there, her own breasts began to swell and ache. They'd done this frequently over the past few weeks. It had troubled Amelia only sometimes. She'd chalked this and so many other things up to her anxiety and stress at work. Already, she'd had a meeting with her therapist, who'd discussed with her various ways she could potentially cope with her inability to receive love and deal with her everyday stress.

Maybe she wasn't such a lost cause, after all.

Mandy and Amelia spoke lightly as they walked: about the upcoming months, about rescheduling the doctor's appointment, and about how they would finally tell Daniel the truth. Mid-way through their hike, Mandy's phone rang. It was her father, so she pocketed it to ignore it. Minutes later, Daniel called Amelia instead.

"I have to get this," Amelia said sadly. "I'm sorry."

"Amelia! Hey!" Daniel sounded bright and happy, the way

people sounded before they learned about news that would change their lives for good.

"Hey, Dan. What's up?"

"Just curious if you'd heard anything from Mandy. She didn't come home from school, and I can't get ahold of her."

"She's with me, Danny," Amelia said. "We're just on a hike. She probably didn't hear her phone."

Mandy grimaced and turned her eyes to the muddy ground below.

"You girls are like two peas in a pod," Daniel replied. "At least I know she's safe. Thanks again, sis."

Although they were only half-way through the trail, Mandy insisted she was too tired to keep going. They rounded back and headed to the car, where Mandy sat forlornly and held her elbows with her hands. Amelia drove them back to her place, where she prepared them fruit smoothies. Mandy stared listlessly at the television.

"I have something for you," Amelia told her. She stepped toward a little baggy, where she procured the classic, *'What to Expect When You're Expecting.'*

Mandy looked at it like it was a ticking time bomb. Amelia pressed it into her hands, then said, "I think the only thing we can do in this life is prepare. Don't you?"

Mandy opened the book to read about pregnancy at six weeks.

"It's funny to read this," Mandy said with a dry laugh. "I could write all this myself. Eight weeks pregnant means PMS symptoms, fatigue, sore breasts, morning sickness. Blah blah. Oh, but wow. My baby is teensy — the size of a kidney bean. Huh."

This was the first time Amelia had heard Mandy refer to the baby as "my baby." This felt like a step forward.

"Oh, my God." Mandy swallowed.

"What?"

"My baby's heart has already begun to beat," she said. Her eyes shone.

"Wow," Amelia murmured.

They held the silence for a moment as though they could hear the baby's heartbeat from beyond.

Suddenly, Amelia had the urgent need to pee. She rushed to the bathroom and fell back on the toilet as her stomach swelled with a cramp. When she returned to the living area, Mandy had placed the book back on the coffee table and begun to gather her things. Her hands shook. Maybe the book had been too much.

"I just want to go rest, I think," Mandy said.

"You should take the book with you," Amelia said.

"I don't know. I don't want Dad to see it," Mandy returned.

Amelia insisted on driving Mandy back home. From the car, she waved to Daniel, who spoke to someone on the phone and was therefore too busy to see the forlorn face of his eldest as she slipped past him.

Back at home, Amelia sat on the couch and glared at the baby book. Several words Mandy had read continued to play out in the back of her mind. Finally, she lifted the book and began to read back some of the symptoms — nausea, fatigue, breast tenderness and pain.

It couldn't be. It really couldn't be.

Amelia grabbed her phone and called Jennifer. She answered on the third ring.

"Hey, babe. What's up?"

Amelia bit hard on her tongue and then found the words.

"Do you think I could be pregnant?"

Jennifer laughed aloud. "Um. What?"

Amelia splayed her hand over her chest to feel the steady thud-thud of her heart. "I have all the symptoms. Of a pregnant woman, I mean. And I don't think I got my period. Actually, I'm sure I didn't."

"But you hardly ever, you know."

"But I did—over a month ago. Remember? Walk of shame and all that?" Amelia said.

"You did do the deed. That's for sure." Jennifer paused for a moment, then asked, "Didn't you use protection?"

Amelia thought back to that crazy impulsive, frantic, strange night with Nathan Gregory. She remembered something, a conversation about protection. And surely, they'd used something. They definitely had. One time, at least.

"We did. I think the first time," Amelia said.

"But how many times...?"

Amelia didn't answer. She'd entered full-on panic mode, now.

"All right, hun. Wow. Okay." There was the sound of a printer, maybe the one at the bakery that printed receipts; Amelia could practically see Jennifer at the register, her eyes wide with this sudden, potential news. "I'm leaving the bakery right now. I'll pick some supplies up on the way."

"Probably it's just in my head," Amelia said. "It's totally not possible."

"Right. It's probably in your head," Jennifer returned. "Like when Mila thought she was pregnant after making out with a guy too much our sophomore year."

Amelia chuckled, then hung up the phone and wrapped her arms around her chest with panic. She fell to the side and stared at the blank glare of the television. Maybe if she'd had even a bit of sense, she would have turned the thing on, just to take her mind off of things.

When Jennifer arrived, she just walked through the front door like she owned the place. Amelia needed that kind of authority just then.

Jennifer placed several pregnancy test strip packages on the coffee table and then lifted up *What To Expect When You're Expecting*. "Why do you already have this?" she asked.

Amelia buzzed her lips. "It's a long story." Still, she wouldn't tell anyone Mandy's secret.

"Well." Jennifer splayed her hands across her thighs. "All I can say is this. You can lay there on your couch, freaking out all night long if you want to. Or, you can take one of these pregnancy tests and find out the truth."

"You're always so logical, Jennifer," Amelia said as she rose up and gripped one of the tests.

"Actually, I'm not. You're normally the one who's logical," Jennifer returned.

Just before Amelia entered the bathroom, Jennifer stepped up behind her and added, "Amelia. Wait."

Amelia turned around and gazed at her dear friend, bleary-eyed. "Yeah?"

Jennifer furrowed her brow. "You know that no matter what

happens, we have your back. Right? Regardless if it's positive or not and what you choose to do afterward."

Amelia let a single tear fall. "Thank you for being here today."

"Anytime, babe. You know, I never thought the great Amelia Taylor would have a pregnancy scare."

"And yet, here we are," Amelia said as she slipped the door closed.

After Amelia peed on the stick, she shoved the cap over it and wrapped the entire thing in toilet paper. She then stepped out into the kitchen in a panic while Jennifer practically chased after her.

"Two minutes!" Jennifer called.

But when two minutes passed, Amelia didn't have the strength to look at the thing. She sipped a glass of water and felt the frantic beating of her heart.

"You know, the longer you make yourself wait, the worse it's going to be," Jennifer said.

"But right now, I'm in the middle," Amelia reasoned. "Everything is possible and impossible right now."

"And I'm starving. If you don't want to look at the pregnancy test now, then I have to insist we order a pizza in the meantime," Jennifer said.

Amelia scrunched her nose. "I can't imagine eating anything right now." She then pushed the pregnancy test across the counter and said, "Will you look? Please?"

Jennifer's lips formed a circle. "Are you sure you want me to know before you?"

"The thought of looking right now makes me want to throw up."

Jennifer heaved a sigh, grabbed the pregnancy test, and turned around so that Amelia couldn't see her. Amelia strained to get some guess of the results from Jennifer's shoulders, but Jennifer gave almost no sign with her body. The silence stretched between them, so much so that Amelia thought her heart would explode.

"Well?" Amelia demanded.

When Jennifer turned back, her eyes shone with tears. They were earnest tears, tears of happiness and the impossible joy of the new. Amelia felt it, deep in her gut, this time.

Against all odds, she was pregnant.

Jennifer placed the positive stick on the counter between them. She then reached across and gripped Amelia's hand, even as it shook.

"You are going to be the best mother of all of us," Jennifer said softly. "This baby is so lucky to have you."

CHAPTER TWENTY-ONE

THE FOLLOWING morning at her office computer, Amelia did something she hadn't done for weeks: She Googled Nathan Gregory. The first results were all linked to him and not some other Nathan Gregory, which told her just how important and rich he was. She clicked through his website and then found a number of photographs of him, all taken at various high-roller functions. In each, he wore that smile that seemed very similar to a sneer, and his eyes seemed to reflect the feeling that he was much, much better than you and he couldn't wait to prove just that. She was sure that if she looked up the word "arrogant" that his picture would be right there.

Still, the genes were strong. Amelia couldn't shake that thought. It would be a big test of nature versus nurture: could she raise an upstanding, kind, and generous individual, even when he or she looked like a god or goddess?

That moment, Oliver Krispin appeared in the crack of her door.

With a sudden smack, Amelia closed her computer and blinked at him, wide-eyed. She knew she acted like a crazy person; she just couldn't help it.

"Hey!" he said. "Sorry. I didn't mean to frighten you."

"What's up?" Amelia said. She tried to smile but felt her cheeks failing her.

"I wondered if you were ready? We were going to meet up with that contractor and then head over to the site?"

Another version of Amelia would have never, ever, not in a million years, forgotten something like this. But this was pregnant Amelia, and apparently, pregnant Amelia had very different rules.

"Of course," Amelia replied as if everything was normal. "Let me just grab my jacket."

Oliver drove them out to the site. Throughout the drive, he spoke about how beautiful Martha's Vineyard was in the spring, that you could feel the excitement as it bubbled forth, with everyone looking toward summer and all summer would be. Amelia, who would have normally been a sucker for this kind of conversation, hardly had anything to say in response.

"I do love summer," she finally said, after a strange moment of silence.

"You feeling okay?" he asked as he parked the car off to the side of the grounds he'd purchased.

"Yeah. I just had a little stomach bug this morning. Sorry," Amelia said.

"We can reschedule this meeting if you want to," Oliver said.

Amelia's heart swelled. It was such a tender thought that someone wanted to go out of their way to make things more comfortable for her. But she shook her head. "No way. We're already here, and we need to stay on schedule."

Throughout the meeting with the contractor, Amelia could feel Oliver's eyes upon her. They both took notes, and both asked relevant questions, but to Amelia, there seemed something else between the two of them, something that simmered in the air. When she checked her notes, as the contractor left the site, she was surprised to feel as though she hadn't been the one to write them. It was like she hadn't been there at all.

"Want to walk the grounds?" Oliver asked when they were alone.

Amelia nodded. Her throat felt suddenly too tight, although she had managed plenty of conversation with the contractor. As they walked toward the water, her heart thudded, and her mind paced back to that night when they'd been at the diner and she'd thought, in some back alley of her mind, that maybe, just maybe, she had a real crush on Oliver Krispin.

Now, she was pregnant with another man's baby and she wasn't totally sure what to do with her attraction for this man. Probably, she should put it to bed. He certainly was way out of her league, that was for sure.

At the water, Oliver turned back and spread his arms wide. "Can you visualize it?" he asked. His voice was wistful.

Amelia blinked several times and tried to imagine it: the resort that Oliver had helped design, the world that would blossom before them. It would be an ecosystem that merged the natural surroundings with a beautiful pool, a swim-up bar, a restaurant overlooking the water, all attached to the moderately-sized resort, with its high Roman columns and its beautiful bay windows.

"It's certainly going to be something special," Amelia said.

Oliver dropped his hands to his sides and turned his green eyes toward hers. "I'm so impressed with how quickly everything has gone since you got back to work. Some of that red tape you knew how to handle blew me away. I would have collapsed on the ground crying mid-way through."

Amelia chuckled sadly. "If there's anything I know my way around, it's red tape."

"You're a strong woman," he said. "That's for sure."

"And you have an eye for architecture," Amelia said. "We make a pretty good team."

Oliver looked incredulous. She could practically see the compliment as it rolled around his mind. Before a moment could pass, he asked, "I don't suppose you'd like to go to dinner again tonight?"

"Oh, um."

"It's just that, yeah, I love diner food. Apparently, I love it a lot more than I ever let on because I've been back to that diner twice since then. The jukebox is to die for."

"I agree," Amelia said with a laugh.

"But I'd like to take you out somewhere proper. Somewhere with real, linen napkins and fewer fried options."

Amelia knew she should say no. In fact, she felt the NO burst up from her stomach, then fall flat before it came out. She nodded somberly, as though she had just agreed to something much bigger than dinner for two. With every part of her body, she wanted to be with him; and beyond that, she knew that if she spent a night at home, alone in her thoughts, she might scream.

Later that evening, Amelia dressed in a simple black dress and analyzed her stomach in the mirror. There wasn't a single sign of a baby. In fact, she felt she'd lost a bit of weight, probably due to all the stress and vomiting. She donned some lipstick and then nearly jumped from her skin when the doorbell rang.

"Pull yourself together," she whispered.

Oh, but there really wasn't anything like being nervous on a date with a man you liked. At least, this is what Amelia discovered now, as she slipped into the passenger seat of his car and watched as he jumped into the driver's side and revved the engine. Why was it that everything he did, now, made Amelia's heart stir with gladness? It was such a problem, falling for someone. It would have been an enormous difficulty anyway, but now that Amelia was pregnant, she felt each wave of lust for him like a wave of panic.

Eliminate. Your. Feelings. She told herself this, like a kind of mantra, and soon laughed at herself, as clearly, this kind of thing didn't work.

Before she knew it, Amelia found herself at-ease with him again. They sat across from one another at a favorite Italian restaurant of hers. Their table sat between two other couples, and the conversation bubbled and popped around them. Amelia said she had a headache and couldn't drink wine, so Oliver decided to just have one glass with his pasta.

"I can't believe your sister-in-law just left like that," Oliver said somberly. "She sounds awful."

"It really broke me up for a while," Amelia returned as she stirred her pasta round and round her fork. "She was really one of my closest friends. I helped her raise the kids."

"Did she ever say anything about wanting to leave?" Oliver asked.

Amelia shrugged. "She would say things here and there about, like, how exhausting it was to be a mom. Or that sometimes, she wondered whether or not she could have made it in the big city. But I thought all moms said stuff like that. Everyone is curious about lives they might have had if they hadn't made all the decisions they made."

"Of course," Oliver said. "But to leave your kids, just because of some idea..."

"I know," Amelia said. "But to be honest, her leaving made me so, so close with those kids. Jake and Mandy are my world. I don't know what I would have done without them in my life all these years."

Oliver's eyes glowed with intrigue. "I want to meet them."

Amelia laughed, surprised at his sudden answer. "I'm sure they'd like to meet you, too."

"But you said Mandy's a senior? Probably she's about to leave the island," Oliver said.

"Maybe. She hasn't fully decided what she wants to do yet."

Amelia turned her eyes back toward her bowl. Despite thinking she hadn't been so hungry, she'd managed to scrape down her alfredo to the very bottom, where the white sauce pooled up.

"I'm jealous, though. That you have them," Oliver said finally. "I'm sure they show you stuff about this new generation and this new world that I'll never know or experience."

"You know, they do, sometimes. But the closer I get to them, the more I realize that nothing really changes. Not as much as we think it does," Amelia said. "Maybe that's a good thing. Although the problems never really get any easier."

Amelia had never had a more honest and beautiful conversation with a man in her life. Date or no date, whatever this was, she cherished it.

Just past nine-thirty, Amelia gave herself away with a massive yawn. She smacked her hand over her lips as Oliver laughed aloud.

"You don't have to pretend to be awake around me. I know I'm boring," he said, wearing a lopsided grin.

"That's really not it. I've just been so slammed with work. Hardly sleeping," she lied.

Oliver paid the bill and walked Amelia back to the car. As they went, his hand swept against her fingers, and she shivered with excitement. In the car, they didn't speak, as though anything said would mean too much. Amelia felt like a silly teenager with a high school crush.

Don't even think about it, she told herself. You're pregnant.

But at the door, when Oliver said, "I had such a wonderful time tonight," and Amelia lifted her chin, she wanted nothing more than what she got.

A kiss. A beautiful, earnest, open, wonderful kiss.

It was the kind of kiss that lifted her off the ground and told her good things could belong to her if only she reached for them.

When their kiss broke, Oliver's hands swept down her shoulders, toward her hands. He held them for a soft moment as he said, "You're one of the bravest and most passionate people I've ever met."

After that, he left.

Amelia crawled into her bed without bothering to get undressed. She played that same stupid Fleetwood Mac song from the diner, "Everywhere," a few times on her phone as she stared into the darkness. She couldn't dare to dream of this, even though this was all she wanted.

It seemed impossible that suddenly, after so many years alone, she had been given a baby and a new love, all at once.

But how cruel that she'd only be allowed to keep one.

Still, she was grateful, if utterly sad.

CHAPTER TWENTY-TWO

"ARE YOU READY FOR THIS?" Amelia asked. She sat in the front of her car; as Mandy leaned back in the passenger seat, the sonogram lifted so that the light swept through the image of her kidney-bean sized baby. The doctor visit had been a roaring success; everything had seemed in-order, healthy, ready. And the doctor hadn't given even a single word of alarm at Mandy's young age. Instead, she'd said only, "Wow. You must be so excited. What a beautiful time," which was exactly what Mandy had needed to hear.

"I guess I'm ready to tell my dad that I'm a huge disappointment and will have a baby out of wedlock, the year after high school graduation?" Mandy asked as she placed the sonogram back on her lap.

Amelia chuckled. "You do have a way with words. Maybe you should think about being a writer."

"I talked to Chelsea recently," Mandy said then. "About maybe getting a shift at the diner for the spring and summer. Save up a bit of money until I have to, you know, succumb to the big-old belly."

"You don't think it would exhaust you to be on your feet all day like that?" Amelia asked.

"I just want to keep my mind off of things and save up tips," Mandy said. "Maybe next year, me and the baby can head off the island and head to college. Maybe I can join a sorority that has its own daycare."

Amelia nearly snorted at the joke. She turned off the engine just outside of Daniel's house, then watched as Mandy eased out from the passenger side. She slipped the photo of the baby into her journal, where, she had told Amelia, she'd started to record some of the strange thoughts and fears she had surrounding pregnancy and motherhood. Although Amelia hadn't told Mandy about her own pregnancy, she'd begun her own journal.

In fact, just that morning, she'd written: *Will I be too old of a mom? What if I can't keep up? What if everyone thinks I'm my baby's grandmother instead of the mother? What if?*

Somehow, writing out these thoughts kept the panic at bay. She acknowledged them and then let them pass. This was something her therapist had instructed her on. Even though Amelia had given her therapist a number of details about her life, she hadn't yet broken the "real" news. That brought with it its own level of therapizing, she supposed.

When they entered Daniel's house, they entered a warm ecosystem of pizza smells and vibrant laughter and Jake's speaker system, blaring a song he wanted to show his dad. Amelia and Mandy walked into the kitchen to find Jake in the throes of air guitar while Daniel nodded along with the beat. Daniel waved and called, "Sorry! Didn't hear you come in!"

"I wonder why!" Amelia laughed.

They paraded into the dining room as Jake switched up the music to something more suited to the background. Amelia sat next to Mandy, whose face was the color of porcelain.

"Eat up, girls," Daniel said. "We have a big night planned. Jake wants to watch two sci-fi movies."

"Try to stop us, Mandy," Jake joked. "Just try to force one of your romcoms on us and see what we do."

Mandy made no motion for a slice of pizza. Amelia's heart thudded as the moment approached. She'd thought maybe Mandy would wait until after dinner. Maybe she was too nervous to eat.

"Dad. I have something to tell you," Mandy said finally.

Daniel held his pizza aloft, near his lips. "What's up, honey?"

Mandy heaved a sigh. Beneath the table, Amelia gripped her hand, which resulted in Mandy clinging to her fingers so hard, she thought her bones might break. Daniel seemed to notice the hand-holding because he dropped his pizza to the plate beneath it and asked again.

"What's up?"

Mandy cleared her throat. After another pause, her dad interjected.

"Did you decide where you're going to college?"

Mandy let out a strange laugh. "Not quite."

"What do you mean, not quite?" Daniel demanded. His eyebrows lowered.

Gosh, this was difficult to witness. Jake had decided to read the top of the pizza box over and over again as a way to escape the situation.

"I'm pregnant," Mandy finally said.

The words were like a bomb going off. Jake actually started to cough, like he wanted to hide the words from reality. All the color drained from Daniel's face. He stared down at his uneaten slice of pizza as though it might come to life and walk across the table.

"You're pregnant," Daniel said finally.

In her entire life, Amelia had never heard her brother sound more disappointed. It was a horrible sound. It was the sound of metal on metal or nails on a chalkboard.

Daniel placed his hands over his eyes. "I just don't understand how you could do this to yourself, Mandy. How could you be so — so — irresponsible?"

These words were more of an attack. Mandy's face grew blotchy with embarrassment. Jake stopped coughing and lifted a slice of pizza to his lips.

"Come on, Daniel," Amelia said suddenly. "Don't be so harsh."

Daniel dropped his hands to the table and balked at her. "Excuse me?"

Amelia shrugged. "Your daughter is here trying to tell you about a huge milestone in her life, and you want to ridicule her. Just think about how much courage she needed to be able to do this in the first place."

Daniel's face turned animalistic and angry. He looked at her like she was a stranger.

"I guess you've known about this all along, huh, Aunt Amelia?" he demanded.

Amelia crossed her arms over her chest and glared at him.

"What does it matter how long I've known? You know now. We all know."

"Mom and Dad don't know," Daniel returned. "What the hell are they going to say?"

"I can guess what Mom will say," Amelia returned. "Something a whole lot meaner than what you did. And it's up to us, Daniel, to help Mandy during this stage of her life. It's up to us to make sure she gets through."

"But Amelia, I'm her father. You shouldn't have kept this from me all this time."

"But I love Mandy like she's my daughter," Amelia interjected. "And more than that, I couldn't very well give over her secrets. She's eighteen years old, and she's about to be a mother. We owe her some respect."

Daniel again turned his eyes toward Mandy, who continued to glower at her journal. After another moment, Mandy brought out the image of her child and swept it across the table toward her father.

"It's real, Dad. Whether you like it or not, this is really happening."

Daniel lifted the photo toward the light. He shook his head slowly and ticked his tongue against the roof of his mouth. When he dropped the photo to the table, he again turned his eyes toward Mandy.

"What about all the things we planned for, Mandy? What about everything we talked about?"

Mandy's cheeks reddened with shame. She looked more miserable than Amelia had ever seen her.

"Daniel, please. We can't have the regret talk right now,"

Amelia returned. "And you know that everything happens for a reason. You said it yourself, almost every day after Suzy left."

Now, it was time for Daniel to glower at Amelia instead. She narrowed her eyes as she said, "You can belittle me or talk down to me or stare at me like that all you want. Just don't do it to your daughter."

"How dare you bring up Suzy in all this?" Daniel demanded.

"Because she's not here, Danny," Amelia returned. "And we are. All of us. Here at this table. Do you know who else is here? Mandy's baby."

"This all shouldn't be up to you, Amelia," Danny offered. "It's like Mom always says. You'll only ever kind of, sort of get the whole parenthood thing. You never tried to do it yourself, so you're just like, peeking through the window and making up your own rules. You're—"

"Actually, I'm pregnant, too, Danny," Amelia blurted out. "What do you say to that?"

Silence fell over the table yet again. Mandy's eyes bugged out of her skull as she took in full view of Amelia. Jake's jaw had dropped toward the ground. In the distance, Jake's speaker system had begun to play Smash Mouth, as though the entire night wasn't just a bad dream.

"You're pregnant?" Daniel exhausted. "What the hell?"

"Language, Dad," Mandy returned, with all of that teenage sass.

Daniel placed both hands over his eyes. "I don't know whether to laugh or cry or both." Slowly, he stood from the table, left his pizza behind, and traced steps back toward his bedroom, the same one he'd once shared with Suzy all those years ago.

Jake took this opportunity to place five slices of pizza on a plate and hustle out of there, too.

This left only Amelia and Mandy — the pregnant women of the Taylor family.

"You have to be kidding me," Mandy finally whispered. She turned her face fully toward Amelia and shook her head. "You really went all-in on your support of me, didn't you?"

Amelia laughed and dropped her chin to her chest. She exhaled deeply, then whispered, "The worst is over, now. He'll get over it. And very soon, he'll know just what to do to support you. You just have to give him time."

"Time. I guess I have that," Mandy said softly. "About seven months, now."

"I guess I have about eight," Amelia returned, smiling.

"Here we go," Mandy said.

"You can say that again."

CHAPTER TWENTY-THREE

"I JUST DON'T KNOW exactly how I feel about it." Anita Taylor's words buzzed through the loudspeaker as Amelia smeared lotion across her cheeks and her forehead. "Imagine. A grandmother, at my age!"

"You've been a grandmother for years, Mom," Amelia returned. "I think you can manage it."

"I just don't know what to do with myself," Anita said. "I just. Well." She paused for a long time. For a moment, Amelia thought maybe they'd lost connection. "I'm just honestly so thrilled for you, Amelia. So thrilled."

Amelia stopped smearing her lotion and gave herself a good, hard look in the mirror. Of course, she'd told her mother the news in-person, but the words had shocked Anita so profoundly that she'd asked Amelia to leave so that she could think about it. This was her, now, calling her back. And it seemed she'd come around. Amelia supposed people in the Taylor family always came around in some way. Everyone needed to take their own time. In Amelia's case, for example, she had needed a full forty years to figure out her life enough to actually make big things happen.

"You'll be a great mother," Anita went on. "I've watched you all these years with Jake and Mandy and thought to myself, what a shame that she never did that. Now, I suppose you will. But you'll do it alone. That's a tragedy."

"It isn't really a tragedy, Mom," Amelia said. "I've done everything else on my own. Why not this, too?"

Anita broached the subject of Mandy's pregnancy after that. She didn't sound particularly pleased, but she did say, "Well, another baby is never a bad thing, is it? And I suppose your two babies will have a funny story to tell twenty years from now. Oh, and you and Mandy can help each other. Goodness, I ask myself, where did the Taylor family go wrong, with two single mothers out there now? But, well. We'll all be there for one another. Won't we?"

A bit annoyed but still overwhelmed that she had even acknowledged any amount of happiness, Amelia eventually got off the phone to prepare the house for the evening ahead. Jennifer, Anita, Jason, Daniel, Jake, and Mandy were still the only people in her world who knew about the pregnancy, which meant one thing: it was time to tell the other Sisters of Edgartown.

Camilla, Jennifer, Amelia, Olivia, and Mila gathered in a circle in Amelia's kitchen. Everyone poured wine and gossiped and complimented one another's outfits; everyone seemed bright and lively and eager for summer. All the while, Amelia sipped diet coke and tried her best to fall into the banter.

It didn't take long for Camilla to blurt, "You seem off tonight, Amelia. Want to tell us what's up?"

Amelia felt her blush creep up from her neck, over her cheeks, and toward her ears. She locked eyes with Jennifer, who gave her a firm nod of encouragement.

"Do you remember that one-night stand I had last month?" she finally said.

"Right! That walk of shame you did," Camilla said. "Can't believe it, still. I wish I had a photograph."

"Yeah. The walk of shame. Well, it turns out, I got a whole lot more out of that one-night stand," Amelia winked as she dropped her hand over her stomach and nodded.

The girls absolutely freaked out after that. There was yelling; there was crying; even Jennifer seemed wild, as though, now that the other sisters knew, she was allowed to fully celebrate. They made multiple cheers; they hugged and whispered and made

promises, like, "Any time you need a babysitter, you have to call me," or, "Oh my gosh, if you need anyone for your lamaze classes, just call me," or, "Oh, I have the perfect ointment for the skin around your belly. It's going to stretch and stretch. Let me bring it for you next time. Although, now that I think about it, it's about twenty years old, isn't it? I'll buy you a new bottle."

Amelia felt wrapped up in love and comfort. She fell upon the couch between Camilla and Olivia, who wrapped her up in a blanket and continued to gab and gossip with the others into the night. Amelia felt sometimes lost in thought, other times hopeful. Regardless of everything, she was grateful to be surrounded by these marvelous hearts — women who would see her through to the end, no matter what.

THE FOLLOWING MORNING, Amelia locked her office door and then sat at her desk to dial a faraway number. The phone blared out four times, then five, until a deep, confident voice answered. It was clear when he spoke that he had no idea whose number this was, which meant he'd deleted it.

"Hello?"

"Hi. Nathan Gregory?"

"Speaking."

"Hello. My name is Amelia Taylor. We a little over a month ago. When you, um, ran into my car."

"Oh! Right. I heard that my insurance took care of all of that. Any problems?"

"No. No problems," Amelia offered. She then swallowed the lump in her throat. "Any problems on your end?"

"No..." He sounded annoyed. He was probably between meetings, or on vacation with a luscious blond, or something equally important.

"Anyway. You probably want to know the reason I'm calling," Amelia said.

"Would be beneficial for me, yeah."

Amelia's stomach dropped. She splayed her hand across the base of it and thought of the baby growing inside of her.

"I just wanted you to know that I'm pregnant."

There was silence on the other line, so much silence that Amelia thought perhaps she'd gone deaf.

"Are you keeping it?"

Amelia felt the words like a smack across the face. After all her years being single, alone on the planet, why would she ever even consider such a thing?

"Of course."

"Okay." Nathan cleared his throat. "Interesting. Well. I should tell you, Amelia, that I already have kids. A number of kids and I don't want anymore."

Amelia's stomach felt sour. "I understand."

"But if this is what you want, you should do what you want."

"I didn't call for your permission," Amelia said coldly. "I just thought you should know, since, you know, this is your baby who's going to walk around in the world."

Nathan chuckled. "I forgot how snarky you could be, Amelia. I liked that about you."

"Glad to hear I made some kind of lasting impression," Amelia returned.

"Sure." Nathan cleared his throat again. He seemed almost chipper, now. "Let me ask you this. Is this really what you want to do? Be a single mother?"

Amelia didn't sense any darkness behind these questions. Rather, Nathan Gregory seemed like a man who studied her for research purposes and nothing else.

"I've never had the chance." Amelia tipped backward in her chair just the slightest bit and stared at the spring sunlight as it danced across the far wall. "If this is my only opportunity, then I guess this is it."

"Well. Guess that morning car accident wasn't our only accident of the day," Nathan said.

She could feel the smile behind his words. Perhaps her baby would be a tiny bit witty, like this man she would never truly know.

"Guess not," she agreed. "Thank God for that."

CHAPTER TWENTY-FOUR

OLIVER KRISPIN GRIPPED the edge of the shovel and stabbed the sharp end into the soft soil. He was draped in light clothing, his dark hair glowing beneath the sun, and when he tossed the shovelful of soil to the side, he lifted his eyes toward Amelia and beamed. This was the ceremonial first shoveling of the grounds. They'd officially broken the seal. Now, the resort would be built from the ground up and Oliver's dreams would be realized.

When he returned to Amelia's side, Amelia's heart jumped into her throat. She hadn't spent much one-on-one time with Oliver in the previous few days, which meant the sight of him now made her even woozier. As the mayor of Edgartown stood to make a speech to the fellow onlookers, Oliver dropped his lips to Amelia's ear and said, "Go to the movies with me tomorrow."

Amelia felt her smile tweak up toward her ears. How could she resist this man?

But as she waited for him the following evening, she couldn't help but draw comparisons from this situation to that of Oliver and his ex-wife, who'd been pregnant with another man's baby. It had broken their marriage. This was the kind of thing that would rip their budding relationship to shreds. Probably, Oliver would never want to see her again.

When Amelia stepped out onto the sidewalk, her eyes found Oliver's, and her heart jumped into her throat. Throughout the drive, she struggled to speak about anything at all, as everything felt beside the point. She'd never wanted to get to the point more in her life.

Oliver bought them popcorn and drinks while Amelia sat in the center of the dark theater, with her hands clasped over her lap. She told herself that she'd give him the news when he got back to his seat; then, when he arrived, he made a joke, and she laughed, and she didn't have the strength again. Perhaps there would never be a right time. Perhaps he could just think she was a bit fat for a few months? Perhaps.

But about forty minutes into the movie, Oliver reached over and clasped her hand. Amelia's heart stopped beating as she turned toward him. She was reminded of long-ago afternoons with teenage boys, who longed to kiss you while the movie went on. As she gazed into his eyes, her mind heavy with this memory, the news just came to her lips. She had to tell him. There was no other way.

"I'm pregnant."

She said the words a bit too loudly so that two people in front of them turned around and hissed, "SHHH."

Oliver's eyes grew wide. He turned his face back toward the film in what looked like complete and total shock. He then placed the barely-eaten bag of popcorn to the side, stood up, adjusted his sweater, and marched out of the theater.

In those horrible moments, Amelia knew it was over.

She hobbled to her feet. She felt totally weak and nauseous, and her boobs ached, and her mind raced. But when she stepped out into the soft light of the evening and gazed up into his eyes, she had this strange feeling — something that told her that maybe, just maybe, everything would be all right.

"Oliver. Can I explain?"

Oliver swept his fingers through his hair. He staggered forward a bit and then returned himself back to her.

"It happened before I ever met you," Amelia murmured. "Just that one-night stand I told you about. I never thought this could ever happen for me, and when I found out, I totally lost my mind. But Oliver, I've always wanted this. To be a mom. And it's not happening the way I always pictured it, but it is happening, and I have to welcome that.

"But then, there's you, Oliver. I didn't expect this at all. I feel things for you that I couldn't have anticipated. But if you don't want to stick around and see where this goes because I'm pregnant, then I have to respect that. I would totally understand that you wouldn't want to be with me, in fact. It's actually crazy to ask."

Oliver held her gaze for a long time. Amelia could almost imagine the words he might choose. She couldn't imagine a single world in which she wasn't totally rejected. Enough of her life had been just a series of rejections, over and over again.

But Oliver reached forward and gripped her hand. His green eyes never lost hers.

"This is messy, isn't it?" were the words he chose. They weren't unkind. In fact, there was something of a joke in their tone.

Amelia laughed slightly. "Ever since we met, it's been a bit messy, hasn't it?"

"From that very first day, I thought, this lady is about to make my life a living hell," Oliver joked.

"And I have. Even now," Amelia said.

Oliver chuckled. His eyes turned out toward the street. They seemed contemplative yet happy. How difficult it was, Amelia thought now, to ever truly know a person. Just now, she felt so strangely close to this man, whom she'd only met about a month before.

"What is that look for?" Amelia said softly.

Suddenly, he dropped his lips over hers, and he kissed her right there on the sidewalk of downtown Edgartown as countless residents filed past. He kissed her as though nobody else on the planet mattered. He kissed her as though this was the only thing he knew.

When their kiss broke, he said, "I'm totally falling for you, Amelia Taylor."

Amelia's throat nearly closed up. "What does that mean?"

He shrugged slightly. "I have no idea. I guess it just means that I'm not willing to give up on this. Not now."

THEY DIDN'T RETURN to the movie. There was too much to say and too much to feel. Amelia returned to the passenger seat of his Mercedes and allowed him to drive her back to his rental property, there along the Nantucket Sound. He poured her a cup of tea and listened to her as she spoke about her fears and excitement regarding the pregnancy. He asked questions and seemed totally focused. And when the end of the night came, neither of them made any motion to leave.

It was a night of passion and darkness and beauty — one of the best nights of Amelia's life. In every way, Oliver made her feel protected and loved. And when she awoke, as the sunlight from the Nantucket Sound streamed over the bedspread, and Oliver slept on, Amelia felt assurance and wealth.

Perhaps she didn't have to do this all by herself, after all.

Perhaps there was a better way.

CHAPTER TWENTY-FIVE

MANDY SAT at the edge of the chair at the doctor's office with her hands on her knees and her eyes toward the wall. Amelia felt the anxiety and panic rolling off Mandy in waves. Her father and brother were meant to arrive at any minute, and Mandy wasn't entirely sure they would show. The mood at Daniel's house hadn't been exactly kosher the previous few weeks.

"They'll come," Amelia whispered. "They have to."

Mandy grimaced. "Maybe I should stop expecting people to show up for me."

"I think the people who love you will always show up for you," Amelia murmured.

"Well, Colin clearly doesn't," Mandy scoffed. Mandy had broken the news of the pregnancy to Colin, who'd just said, "Leave me out of this," very much in the style of Nathan Gregory.

Both Amelia and Mandy had basically decided to say, "Good riddance" to their baby-daddies. Still, it stung to have this huge intimate thing with someone — deliver their baby into the world, without them wanting to be around for it.

Suddenly, Daniel burst into the room, followed by Jake, who carried a catcher's mitt beneath his armpit. Both of them looked winded as though they'd rushed across town. Their eyes found Mandy just as she burst into tears.

There was something about the love between close family that was so powerful. It just made you weep.

Daniel stepped toward his daughter, who lifted herself into a hug. Jake remained awkward, off to the side, as Daniel splayed his hand across Mandy's hair and whispered, "I'm so sorry, Mandy. I'm so sorry. We haven't been there for you the way we should have been. It won't happen like this. This baby is our family, too."

After Mandy's check-up, Amelia, Mandy, Daniel, and Jake sat out by the pier with ice cream cones. It was a beautiful day in late April, and at the very edge of each breath, you could taste the summer season. Amelia licked at her pistachio ice cream and caught Mandy's eye. The girl glowed — not from the pregnancy, but from the fact that her father and brother had finally given in and shown up for her.

Suzy, her mother, was absolutely nothing to her, now. She was just a fleck of memory. She hadn't stuck around.

"You know, our babies are going to be so close in age," Mandy said to Amelia. "Probably best friends."

"They'll be unstoppable," Amelia agreed. "They'll get into all sorts of trouble together."

"I don't even know what that relationship is. Your baby is technically my cousin. Which means it'll be my baby's first cousin, something?"

"Once removed," Daniel affirmed.

"Apparently, your dad has a talent for family trees," Amelia said with a laugh.

"Actually, Mom told me that this morning," Daniel said. "And she wants us all to go there for family dinner tonight if you can manage it. I know Grandma hasn't been the most supportive so far, but I think she wants to be. She's going to do her best."

Just then, Amelia heard her name across the winds. She stood and spotted Oliver, out on his sailboat, with his hand whipping wildly through the air. He beamed at her, and his green eyes reflected back all the love that brewed within him.

"Is he coming to meet us?" Mandy asked.

"I think he is," Amelia said, watching as Oliver tied up his boat and stepped out onto the dock. He then reached down into the boat and drew up two bouquets of flowers.

Oliver approached with windswept hair, his eyes alight. When he reached them, he stepped first toward Mandy and handed her the first bouquet of lilies. She blushed and wrapped her hands around the base.

"Thank you," she said.

"I heard you have prom this next weekend," Oliver said.

Mandy nodded as she wrapped a strand of hair around her ear. "It's going to be a little bit different this year. Aunt Amelia and I picked out a dress the other day. Luckily, I'm not showing so much yet. Not that the whole school hasn't caught wind of it."

She paused as she dropped her eyes toward the ground in shame. Amelia wanted so desperately to translate just how little shame she should have felt for this!

"But a guy friend agreed to take me, you know, despite everything," Mandy finished.

"You mean, someone who loves you a great deal as a person wants to spend a night of dancing with you, about a month before your high school career ends," Amelia corrected. "It's a beautiful thing. He didn't ask you as a consolation. You're one of the greatest catches, Mandy Taylor, and don't you forget that."

Mandy gave her a genuine smile. "Something like that."

Oliver then turned back toward Amelia. He wrapped a strand of hair around her ear, then pressed her bouquet of lilies into her hand. When he spoke, his words were only loud enough for her, especially as Daniel, Mandy, and Jake fell into their own conversation.

"I thought of you all morning out there on the water," he said. "I dreamed that I taught your son or daughter how to sail. I dreamed that I never had to call anywhere but Martha's Vineyard home, ever again."

Amelia could hardly believe her ears. As a blush crept across her cheeks, she said, "You're an old sap, aren't you?"

"Guilty as charged," Oliver said. "Now, how about you sail off into the sunset with me? I'm parked right over there."

Amelia chuckled. "I'll do it. On one condition."

"Anything."

"We have to be home in time for dinner. My mother is dying to meet you. And she doesn't like it when we're late."

Oliver's smile grew wider. "You want me to meet the famous Anita Taylor?"

"If you're brave enough, I think it's time."

Amelia and Oliver told the others they would meet them at the

Taylor house later that evening. Then, Amelia slipped her fingers through Oliver's and allowed him to guide her down toward the dock, where she watched him yank the huge white sail into the wind. It whipped them out across the Nantucket Sound waters. And in mere moments, she closed her eyes and lifted her chin to drench her face in the late-April sun.

OTHER BOOKS BY KATIE

The Vineyard Sunset Series

Secrets of Mackinac Island Series

Sisters of Edgartown Series

A Katama Bay Series

Made in the USA
Monee, IL
12 September 2021